DEATH IN THE PINES

DEATH IN THE PINES

AN
OAKLEY
TYLER
NOVEL

Thom Hartmann

ACADEMY CHICAGO PUBLISHERS

Copyright © 2015 by Thom Hartmann
All rights reserved
Published by Academy Chicago Publishers
An imprint of Chicago Review Press Incorporated
814 North Franklin Street
Chicago, Illinois 60610
ISBN 978-0-89733-761-8 (cloth)
ISBN 978-0-89733-749-6 (paperback)

Library of Congress Cataloging-in-Publication Data
Hartmann, Thom, 1951–
    Death in the pines : an Oakley Tyler novel / Thom Hartmann.
        pages ; cm
    Summary: "Former PI Oakley Tyler finds himself going up against suspicious
locals and big business in the forests of Vermont"— Provided by publisher.
        ISBN 978-0-89733-761-8 (hardcover) — ISBN 978-0-89733-749-6
(softcover) 1. Genetic engineering—Fiction. 2. Murder—Investigation—
Fiction. I. Title.
    PS3558.A7142D43 2015
    813'.54—dc23
                                                    2014036640

Interior design: PerfecType, Nashville, TN

Printed in the United States of America
5 4 3 2 1

To Louise, for decades of love, inspiration, and collaboration, from our teen years to today and beyond . . .

And to DeWitt Wannamaker, who accompanied me through coursework at the Georgia Police Academy, helped me earn my PI license and badge, and is one of the finest law enforcement officers I've ever known. Keep the bagpipes going, DeWitt; you're doing G-d's work . . .

1

You had to be crazy to do this. On a morning when the Vermont winter sun shone pale and weak across six crisp inches of fresh snow, when the temperature hovered somewhere between twenty and twenty-five degrees Fahrenheit, I spent a long time searching for ten stones.

They had to be the right stones, of a certain weight and shape: heavy, but not so heavy they exhausted me, rounded, but not so much so that they would roll from the place where I set them. It took hours to find all ten of them, searching in the sheltered places where the dry, powdery snow was easier to scrape aside. Then they had to be lugged to the spot I had selected, mindless beast-of-burden work that made me sweat inside my down-lined jacket. I stacked the stones carefully into a hollow, truncated pyramid. Anyone coming across that pile of stones in ten or a hundred years would know they weren't dropped there haphazardly by a retreating glacier. This was a made thing, too small to be a cairn, too insignificant to be the remnants of a wall.

I guess you could call it an altar.

The ashes were in a bronze urn, far too small to contain the spirit of my friend John Lincoln. The container had stood on the shelf in my cabin for too many months. The new year had just arrived, and with it a belated first snowfall of the season, and the combination of the two had finally persuaded me it was time to do something about the urn. Holding it in the chill near-silence of the forest, I stood over the structure I had made and looked off into the distance, seeing but not seeing the brownish shafts of pines streaked with snow, the bare gray trunks of maples, the white-and-gray columns of birch, the deep shaded greens of white-burdened firs. At that moment the urn felt heavier than the stones themselves.

This was why I was here.

The mind drifts at such times. Even after six years I could recall the particular night that had caused me to travel to this place. On that night my mentor—no, by that time my friend—John and I had been slumped in the rotting front seat of an ancient, rusting '55 Ford, parked in the heavy, humid midnight of Central America. Despite the choking reek of insect repellent, voracious mosquitoes whined in through the open windows, and from time to time we slapped an offender, reducing it to a moist crumple of tissue to be flicked off a fingertip. Still warmer than blood heat even at that hour, the dark air sizzled with cicadas. We had left our home base in Atlanta a week before and had taken a circuitous route to this dark clearing hacked from jungle. We were waiting for either three or four men to emerge from a blacked-out warehouse, and we had no idea whether those men knew we were watching or how well they might be armed. What we would do depended on how many came out: if only three, we would move in and recover what had been stolen. Four would make the recovery problematic, because that would mean that at least one of the men would be a local, complicating the calculus of violence.

As I stood over the stone altar, every detail of our conversation went through my mind, a tape rewound and replayed. By that point in our lives, John and I had been partners for so long that we didn't bullshit each other, had no need to strain for machismo, no use for phony heartiness. We were a good team. We could finish each other's sentences, catch body-language signals that amounted to a silent code, recognize unspoken concerns and anxieties in time to be prepared for the unexpected. We'd told all our jokes to each other years before. Once in a while one of us might mutter two or three words of a punch line. The other would chuckle in appreciation or exasperation, as the mood took him.

That night in stop-and-start fashion we each spoke of good times we'd had. Waiting in the dark gave each of us a natural urge to talk. That was the one and only time that John had spoken in his quiet way of the forested hills of Vermont, thinking of the coolness of a New England autumn in that hellish tropic night. I had never known that he had been to Vermont. He had lived in Buckhead, a suburb of Atlanta, the whole time I'd known and worked with him. But in those suffocating hours of darkness, cool green Vermont was on his mind. "Beautiful place, very peaceful," he'd said. "I'd like to go back there when it's all over."

I didn't have time then to ask what he meant or when *what* would be over—the job, the summer, the career, the life. At that moment dim yellow light from a kerosene lantern appeared on the black face of the warehouse, first a line, then a thin rectangle, then a fat square as the three men inside pushed open the double doors. John and I climbed out of our borrowed car and did our job.

In the six years that followed that night, John never had gone back to Vermont, had never even spoken of it again, and now for him it really was all over. After the memorial service, after the will was probated, I didn't feel like hanging around Atlanta, so I made arrangements, gave most of my liquid assets to a community for abused kids in New Hampshire, and bought a cabin on two hundred acres in the woods of Vermont. It was here I'd brought my old friend to the place he had talked about. Pondering the finality of it all, I held the urn containing his ashes, a few bone fragments, and pieces of his teeth, ready to fulfill a promise I had never made.

Such a time demands words. I took a deep breath of icy air and looked up toward the top of a towering birch. A squirrel had made an untidy, tangled nest up there in the highest branches, and the animal itself—or maybe another squirrel, who could tell?—hung below the nest, head-down on the trunk, apparently gazing at me. I imagined the squirrel's bright black eye held accusation. The fall had gone on so long, probably for half of the animal's lifetime, so what was the idea of all this snow? Was I to blame?

Clearing my throat, I reached far back into memory, groping for the prayers I had last recited as a child. I heard myself say, "Dear God." My words took flight toward the washed-out sky on puffs of vapor. As far as I could tell, no one heard them but me and the squirrel. My voice had a harsh tone even to my own ears, a rusty-hinge catch. "Whoever, whatever is there. Spirits of the forest, of the living world, whatever. My good friend John has come to rest here. Take care of him." I opened the urn and shook the contents out, over the pyramidal altar and on the bare earth around it—the place I'd scraped free of snow.

Human ashes are as gray and coarse as cement mix. In the frigid, still air of January the mortal remains of John Lincoln pattered down, not drifting at all, falling straight as sand trickling through an hourglass. I emptied the urn, then set it down inside the open center of the hollow pyramid. The last stone covered it and completed the altar. "Take care of him," I repeated, and in the silence I added, "And tell me just what the hell I'm supposed to do with my life now."

With my gloved hands, I scooped up the loose, clean snow from the edge of the clearing and dropped it down over the pyramid and the place where I'd sprinkled the ashes. More snow would fall, the spring thaw would come sooner or later, the snowpack would melt, and the trickling water would carry the ashes down through the thin soil, down to the stone heart of the hills.

My eyes stung, but not with cold. I took a long breath, gave John a last nod, and turned to trudge up the hillside. Up there past the end of the old logging road, my cabin waited for me, dry and warm and stocked with wine.

2

A little more than two weeks passed with more snow and then a warming, the kind of false thaw that turns the forest wet and sets streams of clear water gurgling just under the snowpack. The air smelled of pine and mulching leaves on the floor of the forest. When I woke up on that deceptively warm morning, I didn't figure it for the kind of day somebody was about to die.

At around three in the afternoon, as I surmised from the shadows on the windows, I sat reading an insider's account of life in the Central Intelligence Agency, noting the many inaccuracies. A sound distracted me: boots crunching in the snow. I set my book aside and reluctantly left my rocking chair in front of the woodstove, faintly irritated at the intrusion. I finished the last of my third glass of wine and stood at the front door, which I had cracked an inch or so to let in fresh air.

Through the opening I saw him, still halfway down the hill. He walked deliberately, an old man in work-faded jeans and paint-spattered brown leather jacket trudging through a snow cover that, away from the protection of the evergreens, had drifted two feet thick. It was a steep half-mile climb from the old logging road, and he breathed hard, rasping out ragged pennants of vapor in the still air.

I didn't want visitors. I was more than eight months along in my latest attempt at retirement. I didn't recognize the man toiling up toward my front door, and that made me want to talk with him even less.

But he wanted to talk to me. Still a hundred feet from the cabin, he roared, "I know you're there, Oakley Tyler!" His voice carried a full load of gravel. "They say you're some kind of hermit, but I think you'll wanna see me." Once he reached the stamped-down snow that was the record of my coming and going on firewood errands, he made better time, and stopped just short of the steps up to the little porch, slightly stooped, chest heaving, getting his breath back.

I pushed the front door open, stepped out onto the porch, and said, "I'm not buying any."

"I'm not sellin' any." He wore a beard, mostly gray and neatly clipped at two inches long, and he had pulled back his half-gray, half-brown hair into a ponytail that fell six inches below his shoulders. The afternoon light made his wrinkled skin look like furrowed cropland seen from the air, his face weathered and his forehead pocked with small, angry pink welts as if he'd been careless frying up a big pan of bacon and had been spattered and burned. The outer edge of his left eyebrow had been heat-frizzled, too, and was much shorter than his shaggy right brow, giving him a kind of off-balance look. Spidery capillaries lent the only vital color to his nose and cheeks, a faint red web under yellow-gray skin. He stood about four inches shorter than my six foot two.

He took in a long breath, then looked from me to the door behind me. "That's not the original door, is it?"

"The original was rotten. I made this one of old barn wood," I told him, surprised that his eye could spot the difference. I had tried for a close match.

He grunted. "Thought you'd be living in a fancier place than this," he said. "This's just an old huntin' camp. Nobody's used it in twenty, twenty-five years." His blue eyes sparkled, although the whites were faintly yellowed.

"It suits me just fine," I said, feeling a touch of self-righteous pride in my simple one-room home, furnished with things I'd bought at the Salvation Army or found at yard sales. "Keeps the taxes low."

The old man chuckled and said, "'I went to the woods because I wished to live deliberately, to front only the essential facts of life, and see if I could not learn what it had to teach.' That it, Tyler?"

I might have pegged him as an old hippie. "I'm not Thoreau," I said. "And this ain't Walden Pond."

One corner of his mouth lifted in a crooked smile and he snorted, a half-laugh. "Maybe not. But a famous detective like you, I figured you'd have a big house. You been wrote up in all the newspapers, even in *Time* magazine, some of the cases you and John Lincoln cracked." He pulled his head back and looked at the forest around us, then back at me. "Although you might have somethin' about the taxes at that. What you got here, about three hundred acres?"

"I don't discuss American literature or my real estate holdings with strangers," I told him, sending him into a spell of guffawing.

"OK, I'm sorry," he said. His blue eyes squinted at me shrewdly. "You're being more hospitable than I expected, at that. Half thought you might meet me with a rifle in your hands."

"Shotgun," I told him. I'd bought one five weeks earlier and had fired it on only one occasion, not killing a thing but just trying the weapon out. "I only bring it out when missionaries come to call." That was a lie, because none ever troubled with the climb up to my cabin, though the fleeting fantasy of sending them packing with a shot over their heads did make me smile.

"Well, I'm not peddlin' Gospel either, son," he told me, glancing down at his splattered black lace-up work boots. "I can understand your being sort of stranger-shy, so let me tell you who I am. Name's Jeremiah Smith. Actually related distantly to Joseph Smith. He was born just about ninety miles from here, you know. Nearly two hundred years ago."

"So you're a Mormon? Maybe I should have picked up the shotgun."

He stepped up onto the porch, and then I could smell his yeasty breath. He looked irritable, no longer the twinkly-eyed ex-hippie. "I ain't no Mormon, and ain't here to bother you with anything like that!" He straightened up, as if reaching for dignity. "I come up to hire you."

"You wasted your time, Mr. Smith. I'm retired."

He cocked his head to one side and squinted his left eye. "The hell you say! You ain't a day over forty."

"Good pension plan," I told him, and turned to go back inside.

His voice stopped me: "Wait! Tyler, listen to me. I need a private eye, or whatever the hell you are, 'cause they're planning to kill my grandson. Now, I know I don't look it, but I got money. I can pay you. It's my grand-boy, Tyler. My only livin' relative."

So maybe the wine had mellowed my mood, or maybe I was tired of sitting indoors for days on end without seeing another human being, only going out to get firewood or to collect snow to melt for water or to use the outhouse.

For whatever reason, I pulled the door open and said, "Come on in out of the cold."

Jeremiah Smith stepped inside and closed the door behind him, stomped the snow off his boots on the rough pine floorboards, and followed me over to the two rocking chairs on the coiled-rag rug in front of the woodstove. I gestured him into the plainer one.

"Ain't really cold," he said conversationally as he settled in. "Gotta be above freezing. Maybe thirty-four, thirty-six degrees. Thank you for hearing me out."

"Glass of wine?" When he nodded, I got an extra glass from the cupboard and filled it and my own. I set the bottle on the floor, next to its empty brother.

As I settled into the other rocker, the bentwood one that I favored, Smith leaned forward, both hands holding his glass, and asked, "How long you been drinkin'?"

"About three hours. Since lunch."

"You don't seem drunk."

I realized Smith had assumed I'd knocked off most of two bottles of wine. I didn't bother to tell him that the first bottle had been emptied the day before. Actually, I drank slowly, just keeping a soft buzz on, reading my book as I alternated glasses of wine with glasses of melted snow-water. I shrugged and said, "I hide it well."

He finally took a sip, tilted his head thoughtfully, and nodded his approval. "Now," he said with an air of getting down to business, "before I tell you about my problem, what is this crap about being retired, Tyler?"

"When the senior partner of my firm died, I packed it in. Decided to leave Georgia and come up to Vermont. I had some savings. I can stretch it out by living simply."

"Simply, yeah," he said, tilting back his glass.

"Or maybe I wanted to front the essential facts of life, Mr. Smith." I completed the quotation from Thoreau that Smith had started outside: " '. . . and see if I could not learn what it had to teach, and not, when I came to die, discover that I had not lived.' "

He chuckled, though his blue eyes held no amusement. "Or maybe you're just brushing me off because they got to you already. You working for Caleb Benson?"

The sharp way he asked it showed that he was trying to startle me into reaction. I shook my head. "Never heard of him. Who is Caleb Benson?"

He stared down into his Merlot, in a crystal-cut juice glass that I'd found at a yard sale for ten cents, and then took a long drink. "It don't matter. Look, let me tell you what's on my mind. Then you decide whether you're retired or not."

"Fair enough."

He was quiet for a few seconds. I couldn't tell whether he was gathering his thoughts or fighting his suspicions. "Senior partner'd be Lincoln, I suppose?"

"Died last spring," I said. "Heart attack. That's as much as you need know." I didn't go into the details. John and I had finished a case for a national corporation, ferreting out the disgruntled employee selling trade secrets. We'd written a hefty report, and then John had turned in early. I'd gone out to a show and dinner with a lady; John had told me he would hand-deliver our report the next morning. He got as far as the lobby of the corporation's headquarters before collapsing. A guard did CPR, the paramedics showed up within minutes, everything that could be done had been done. The hospital cardiologist later told me he'd never known anyone to survive that particular kind of heart attack, unless the patient had already been hospitalized when it hit.

You play the sad, sorry games of guilt with yourself. John had been taking his medications and had been exercising, watching his drinking and his diet. Still, they told me at the hospital, his potassium level had dropped so low that it triggered the heart attack. I should have noticed he looked bad those last few days. I should have talked him into a doctor visit.

I became aware that Smith was reading my expression, or trying to. "Go ahead," I said. "You've got till the end of the bottle, that's all."

He raised his glass. "To retirement," he said. "Nothin' like it." He sipped and then said, "I'm retired, too, you know. I'm seventy-two years old, and I been retired for twenty-two of 'em. Worked for the town of Montpelier for thirty years, starting when I was twenty. Did forestry work for the state on the side, that was always my first love, but for my full-time income I drove the snowplows and repaired streets and put up signs and all kinds of crap. Glad I got out before they brought that damn freeway through. Traffic has gone all to hell."

That made me smile. Montpelier, the state capital about twenty miles away from my cabin, has a population of some ten thousand: it's the smallest state capital in the country, and the only one without a McDonald's, a source of pride to the townspeople and no doubt a cause of angst among the captains of the fast-food industry. Rush hour means it takes eight minutes to drive from one end of town to the other, instead of the normal four.

I shrugged. "I decided not to wait until I'm fifty or sixty. Instead I try to retire as often as I can. Work for a while, make enough money to retire for six months or a year, then work a while again."

"I guess it makes a kind of sense," he said. He watched me pour another glass for myself. "But tell me straight, you on the bottle? You an alcoholic?"

"That's not one of my demons."

"Be careful with it anyway, son. It can sneak up on you." He set down his glass and leaned forward, taking a deep breath. "All right. My demon right now is that I'm pretty damn sure they're gonna kill my grandson, Jerry." His voice sharpened. "Don't ask me for any kind of proof, because I ain't got that. Gettin' it would take your help. Right now, I just know it in my gut. I know that kind of men."

Telling me even that much had cost him effort. He had my curiosity up. "What kind of men?"

Smith leaned back in his rocker then, stretching his neck like an old turtle come to the surface after a winter of hibernation. He stared up into the corner of the ceiling over the door, but his eyes had an unfocused quality, as if he were searching for something far in the distance. "The kind of men," he said slowly, "who think they got the right to play God. Son, you got no idea how big this is."

"What do you want me to do about it?"

"Help me. You watch out for my grandson, work with me for a few days. I can't tell you how to do your job, but you'll see what needs doing. Unless I miss my guess, give a week, ten days, you'll have all the proof we need. You'd know how to use it to stop them. See, Jerry's too young to know what he's gettin' into. He tried talking to them, thought he could pry into their business because he works for the newspaper, freedom of the press and all. He don't understand men like that, but I do, and I expect you do too. He don't realize they'll kill him before they'll let him print a word of any story he puts together. Now before I go any farther, how much you charge?"

"It varies," I said. "But—"

He pulled a handful of folded bills from his jeans pocket. "Call this a retainer?" he asked, handing the money over to me.

He gave me four twenties, a ten, and two fives. I started to tell him that Lincoln and Tyler specialized in big jobs, working for corporations that would pay us more in a day than most people earn in a year, but I never got the chance.

Because at that moment the bomb went off.

3

It sounded as if an artillery shell had exploded in my front yard, rattling the windows and jangling the plates by the sink. Smith sprang up and beat me out the door. From some atavistic instinct—this is my house, I must defend it—I snatched up the shotgun and pelted after him. He was already wading through the break he had made in the deep snow, and beyond him I could see flames licking up into the trees about a half-mile down the mountainside.

"My truck!" he bellowed, not slowing a step.

He was still ahead of me, but not by much, when we reached the blazing vehicle: an old red Chevy pickup, rusted out along the sides, dark green paint on the right front fender. The front driver's side sported a faded bumper sticker that said WE WERE ALWAYS HERE with some smaller type along the bottom that I couldn't read. Flames licked out from beneath the chassis, and the cabin boiled with black smoke that scrabbled like a frantic living thing at the closed windows, seeking escape.

Smith turned toward me with a grim expression. "It's a warning."

I wasn't buying it. Fires happen. "You leave a cigarette burning inside? Anything flammable in the back? Flares, dynamite, anything like that?"

"I don't smoke," he said, "and the bed was empty." He stood about ten feet from the driver's side door and pointed. "Look." The gas cap was missing and the area around it had burned black. The snow and dirt under the truck looked like the tank had exploded downward. "They lit a wick of some kind. It would blow off the fumes in the tank when it burned down low enough. Give somebody time to get away."

"Teenagers," I suggested.

Smith shook his head, ponytail swaying, his face pinched together in a way that accented the frown wrinkles and made his eyes look sad and his mouth angry. "Way the hell out here? That kind of stuff kids do at night, in town, after a few cases of beer."

"Want me to call the police?" I said, pulling my cell phone out of my shirt pocket.

He grunted and spat on the ground near his feet. "No. I've been trying to tell you, Oakley. This's bigger than the little town of Northfield, and, besides, they come out here and it just ends up in the paper and I look like a fool." He swept a lean hand down his face, over his beard, and heaved a sigh. "Lemme call Bill Grinder, he's got a new wrecker. Tow this thing in and see if anything can be done."

I handed him the phone, and as I stepped back, a flicker of motion out in the forest caught the corner of my eye. I looked hard, but could see nothing besides trees. Maybe it was a deer, holding still and now invisible in the underbrush.

After Smith finished his call, he handed the phone back to me and said, "You gonna take this case now? You see what we're up against?"

Both rear tires of the truck had deflated, but they hadn't ignited, and the flames were dying down. I doubted that Smith could use the truck for anything but scrap, but he hadn't asked my opinion on that. I said, "Smith, I'm not even licensed in this state."

"Can't you do a favor for a friend?"

I had to grin at that. "You're a friend?"

"Other than that waitress in town, I expect I'm about the best friend you've got in this state." He returned my grin, though he still had a sick expression on his face.

Somehow he stung me into indiscretion. I protested, "Wanda's a hell of a lot more than just a waitress." That much was true. She had dropped out of grad school to work as a waitress so when her daughter got home from school she could be there for her.

"Speaking as a man who's lived a lot of years and seen a lot of places," Smith said evenly, "don't you think *most* waitresses are a hell of a lot more than a waitress?"

Mousetrapped by an aging hippie. "It's not like that with Wanda and me." I wondered if everybody in town thought we had something going.

Smith laughed once, a sharp, abrupt hoot like a disturbed owl. "Oakley, you're more like me than you wanna admit. You afraid of that? Afraid of turnin' out like me in thirty years? You—God *damn!*"

I heard the bullet ping off the hood of the truck in the same instant that I saw his head jerk and a puff of blood and tissue explode from his ear. The report came maybe a tenth of a second later, and by that time I had grabbed Smith and pulled him to the ground. As we rolled into the ditch, another shot shattered the driver's side window, letting the pent black smoke gush out.

"You OK?" I asked over the soft gurgling of the roadside stream.

"Damn. Just tore up my ear," he said. "Hurts like a bee-sting."

"Stay here and lay low." I moved off in a crouch, shotgun at port arms, heading downhill, where the shooter had to be. Same direction where I'd noticed the flicker of motion. My instincts were not as sharp as they used to be.

I kept to the edge of the logging road until I could duck into the cover of the evergreens, where the going was a little easier. I felt seriously outgunned: I had the shotgun, but whoever had ripped a chunk out of Smith's ear had a rifle capable of firing a slug at supersonic speed.

No sounds. Maybe the shooter thought that Smith was dead, that the job had been finished. I froze and listened. Back up the hill I could hear the tink and creak of the cooling truck. I could see Jeremiah Smith through the trees, but only because I knew exactly where he lay. At any distance, he would look like a boulder shouldering through the snow cover at the edge of the road. Smith was a disciplined man. He moved not at all.

I crouched over and zigzagged from trunk to trunk, looking and listening for any sign. Nothing.

I emerged from the woods at the point where the town-maintained road joined my old dirt logging road. Having covered a quarter of a mile from the truck, I had seen only rabbit, deer, and coyote tracks. Now, looking around, I spotted a place where a hawk or owl had snatched something, probably a chipmunk, and hit the snow with its wings. Deer scat lay where the running snowmelt had broken through into a frigid water hole. The droppings looked like rough, round brown marbles melted into the snow. The delicate tracks of a fox, crisscrossing the area. I spent about a half-hour scouting around without turning up anything more deadly or threatening than that.

Just as I was about to turn back, I heard a splashing in the river on the far side of the road. I followed the sound and picked up the tracks of a man: boots with a deep tread, heading down toward the river.

I walked alongside his trail, keeping a wary scan of the forest ahead. Came to a slight rise, and then there was a steep drop, perhaps a hundred feet, down to the forest floor ten feet this side of the Dog River. I could see where he'd climbed down, where his tracks resumed in the snow, and where they vanished into the shallow water. He could have gone downstream, in the direction of town, or he could have turned the other way, toward the crossroads and the old wooden bridge. Three miles or so by road, maybe a third of that if he followed the river.

Either way he was gone, and I felt the hairs on the back of my neck prickling. Whoever had taken the shot, he had to have seen me coming—hell, I had spent thirty minutes outside of cover just across the road, casting back and forth for his trail. Whoever it was could have shot me before I had even caught sight of him. And the fact that he was willing to wade the frigid edges of the Dog River suggested the man had certain reserves of endurance.

By now I could hear the low growl of a truck coming up the town road, probably Bill Grinder in his wrecker. Dusk was coming on fast, so I crossed the road and headed back to the truck, walking the shortest way toward where the sky was darkest, the northeast, where I knew I'd find my own trail worn into the snow over the past few days, the distinctive scrape marks of snowshoes. I came to a rise, gray slabs of ancient shale stacked untidily, as though God had thrown down a losing poker hand, and climbed the hillside in its lee, where the snow was relatively thin.

And stopped with a jerk when I saw a woman ten feet away from me, sitting on one of the slabs.

She looked at me as if she'd expected me. She must have heard me coming. Small details registered: she was probably ten years younger than I, with long black hair, shiny and clean, a strong-featured face, knife-blade nose, heavy black eyebrows, a smiling mouth, and big, dark smiling eyes. Something, though, was out of kilter, out of focus. Her gaze had an ancient air. She might have been sculpted from the stone.

"Ah," I said, standing there holding my shotgun, feeling foolish.

She inclined her head a little, smiling more broadly, absurdly beautiful in the fading light, and I realized she wore buckskins, shirt and pants. Her long-fingered hands lay one on top of the other in her lap, and she sat cross-legged, like an idol. She wore moccasins, odd boot-like ones that laced up to where they vanished beneath the pant legs. I could see the soles, and they were not only dry but absolutely clean, as if the woman had been dropped down from outer space.

I gestured, stupidly, with the shotgun. "Who are you?"

She blinked her large brown-gold eyes and took a long, deep breath. Her skin was a warm, deep golden-brown. She had high cheekbones and a faint gauntness to her cheeks, as if she'd been eating lean during the winter. When she spoke, her voice was so soft that I had to lean toward her to hear it at all. "My people call me a name you could not pronounce or understand. You might call me . . . Sylvia." She seemed to work at making each syllable and word come out perfectly, as if maybe she'd grown up with a speech impediment or stutter and had overcome it by sheer force of will. Her tone held no apology. Instead, she made me feel obscurely as though I were the intruder, as though an apology might be in order.

But I was thinking like an investigator, too, at some level. We were downhill from where the truck had burned. She might have fired the shot—except she had no rifle, and her moccasins had not left the boot tracks that I had followed.

"You see somebody around here with a rifle?" I asked.

She shrugged, then pointed toward the river with her chin. "There was somebody farther down the hill. I heard two shots. He was hiding in the ditch across the road when you turned toward the town, and then he got up and ran down the hill to the water."

I was wondering how the hell she had planted herself on that rock without leaving tracks herself. The snow uphill from her was thin here in the cover of the woods, but it lay absolutely unmarked. "Did you get any sort of look at him? What he was wearing?"

She held her right hand up and waved it from side to side, as if she were saying "no" with it instead of shaking her head. "It was a man, but I did not see him. I only sensed him."

"And what are you doing here?" I could not keep an edge of frustration out of my voice.

"Just sitting." She smiled, the kind of smile that comes from the stomach and ends up on the face, that moves from one person to another. It touched my irritation like warm wind on snow. "You don't need your weapon," she added. "A bit of food to leave for Squirrel would be better."

"How'd you get here? Why are you here?"

She moved her head, as though indicating the jumbled pile of slate slabs. "My people live near here, and this site was once a holy place of friends of ours. I come here sometimes."

That told me something, anyway. "Are you Abenaki?" I said. Just a week earlier there'd been an article in the paper about an Abenaki burial site being dug up by a developer. The Abenaki Indians had once ranged from Maine to Michigan, but by 1700 few remained alive after repeated encounters with Europeans. By 1800 the census had counted only about a thousand; since then their numbers have increased, and now Abenaki are scattered all over Vermont and in the Adirondacks of New York.

The woman tilted her head, as if considering what she was. "No," she said. "Not Abenaki. My people were here before the Abenaki."

The sun had set, turning the forest into a black-and-white sketch of winter. I heard men's voices and the rattle of a chain, and looked away through the trees, trying to see what Smith was doing. When I turned back, the woman was gone.

I walked all the way around the little hill formed by the stone slabs, but found no trace of her, and no tracks indicating her arrival or departure. Stumped, I hurried back to the logging road.

Jeremiah Smith was standing now and he half-turned to look at me as I came out of the woods. The shiny tow truck had backed up just downhill from the rear of the pickup, headlights throwing yellow cones down toward the road. Somebody was going through the business of getting a chain around the rear axle, probably a difficult job with two flat tires.

From down the slope I heard a kind of hurried clatter and turned just in time to see a doe break from the forest edge and rush in great rocking-horse leaps down the slope toward the road and the river. I couldn't image raising my shotgun.

In the twilight, she was simply too lovely to shoot.

4

A cursing man came worming out from beneath the pickup. He had a brush cut, small ears, eyes that were set too far apart, and a little pig nose much too small for his large, square head. "Think that's got the sumbitch," the man said. "Jeremiah, turn the spot around."

Smith reached to comply. The tow truck's lights, including an impressive spotlight mounted next to the yellow flashers on top, illuminated the immediate area. "Here's Oakley back," Smith said. "Find anything?"

"Tracks," I said. "Across the road, leading from the river and back there again. He walked from just below here into the woods, took his shots, then headed down to the river and took off from there."

Smith nodded. "Ain't no amateur. Sure ain't no kids, like you thought." He nodded at the man who had just hooked up his truck. "This is Bill Grinder."

Bill Grinder wiped his big red hands on a bandanna that might have been scarlet when it was new, took the cigar out of his mouth, flipped a lever and winched the rear wheels of the pickup a few feet off the ground, then put an iron brace in place. "Jeremiah says somebody shot him," he said to me, half a question half a challenge, as he walked over and stood with us.

"Looks that way," I said. In the harsh light, I could see that Smith's earlobe was pretty badly ripped up, a ragged hole edged with congealed blood that looked black. He had streaks of dark blood on his neck, a spatter of it on his shirt collar, and some clotted blood matted on his gray beard.

"Jeremiah, I told you already," Grinder said. "Dammit, let me call the cops."

"And I already told you no," Smith said. "It'd just make the papers and I'd have every snoopy bastard in town at my door, and they couldn't do a damn thing anyway. He got away."

"Shootin' folks's a crime," Grinder said, speaking around the cigar he had chomped down on again.

"Might have been an accident. A hunting accident," Smith said in a dry voice.

"Deer season's been over for a month." Grinder replied.

Smith gave me a sidelong glance that said as well as words could have that Bill Grinder wasn't the brightest bulb on the tree. "Yeah, but he might have been hunting fox or rabbit. Maybe wild turkey. Some damn thing's gotta be in season now."

Grinder looked at me in frustration. I shrugged and he shook his head and sighed, breath like the breeze off a dung-heap, not sweetened any by the stogie he sucked on. "Oh, hell, it's your problem. Guess it was just an accident like you say, Jeremiah. You gonna ride into town with me?"

Smith raised his lopsided eyebrows at me in inquiry and I said, "Up to you. I've got a Jeep, can take you in later, or you can call for somebody to pick you up. Maybe you should have a doctor look at that ear."

He snorted at the suggestion. "You got rubbing alcohol and a Band-Aid?"

"I have."

He turned to Bill. "I'll stay on here a bit. We got some talkin' to do."

"Suit yourself," Grinder said. He took his cigar out, spat, and jammed the slimy butt back into his mouth as he walked around the front of his tow truck, got in, and drove off slowly. The pickup clattered along behind, looking as dead as a gutted deer.

Back up in the cabin, I put away the shotgun and lit my kerosene lantern. Jeremiah Smith spent five minutes in front of a mirror with the rubbing alcohol and a washcloth and finally decided not to bother with a bandage. "Heals better in the dry air anyhow," he said. "And I'm too old and ugly to worry about that little missing chunk."

He looked out the north side window, then the south side window behind him, then the east facing windows on the front of the cabin. I doubted he could see anything. Deep darkness had settled in. "Only one way out of this place? Don't seem safe."

"You mean if they're still shooting at us?"

He tapped the beam he stood next to. "Or if they set fire to the place. Whatever."

"There's a hinged panel in the back wall," I said, pointing to the wall next to my woodpile. "Hinges on the top, an eyehook on the bottom."

"For putting in wood," he said, catching on at once.

"Yes, but it's big enough to crawl through in a pinch. Meet your approval?"

He shook his head as if at the sorry state of my lodgings, walked over to the straight-backed rocking chair, paused with his hand resting on the hard maple, heaved a deep breath, and said, "You got anything stronger than wine?" He touched the lower part of his ruined earlobe. "Anesthetic," he explained.

"Some vodka in that cabinet under the window," I said. "Should be about full."

He snorted, as if vodka were an absurd idea, and sat down, picking up from the floor his juice glass, still about half-full. He polished off the claret with one swallow. "You ready to believe me now? You ready to work for me?"

"Do you know of any Native Americans living around here?" I countered.

He didn't respond for a minute, but poured himself another glass of wine while he mulled that over. "A few. Why?"

"Just curious. How about a woman in her twenties or thirties named Sylvia?"

He shook his head. "I don't know anyone of that name. They's a few Abenaki around. Also some up north, and in Quebec, and in New York. A few in the Northeast Kingdom, maybe a few scattered round about in Maine."

"Any other tribes around here? Anybody who lived here before the Abenaki?"

Smith shook his head. "Don't know of any tribe could claim that. The Abenaki arrived here when the glaciers receded, around eight thousand or so years ago, and the books all say they was the first humans here. What's this about Indians, anyhow?"

I shook my head. "Not important." The story didn't bear telling, because it sounded too damn odd in my head as I thought it over. I was beginning to wonder exactly who or what I'd seen sitting on that rock. No coat, yet she didn't seem cold. No tracks leading there or away. I glanced at the bread on the counter, wondering if it was moldy. Ergot, a grain mold, can produce lysergic acid, the LS of LSD. The woman had been evanescent enough to be a hallucination. Maybe, I thought, stretching the point, I should be buying bread with some nice, healthy preservatives in it.

"Come on," Smith demanded, leaning forward. "What are you saying? The guy took a shot at me was an Indian, is that it?"

"I have no idea who shot at you," I said, "except that his boots are about a size larger than mine, which is a size ten. So he probably is either wider or taller than me, or maybe both."

"And you're about six foot and, what, one-eighty?"

"Close enough."

Smith shook his head, wincing a little, and I guessed his ear was hurting him more than he let on. "Wasn't no Indian, I can tell you that." He took a huge swallow of the wine.

"You an expert on them?" I said.

He stared at me for a moment, as if I'd just insulted him and he was trying to figure out whether to throw his glass at me or walk out. I held his eyes for five seconds, and then looked down at the rug. After another ten seconds or so, he said evenly, "You got something against Native Americans?"

"Absolutely nothing at all," I said.

"What if some bureaucrat for the state said that the Abenaki or some others had a claim to your land, that you'd have to pay them or give it up? What'd you think then?"

I glanced around the room at the exposed rough wood, the junk-shop furnishings, and said, "I think I could walk away from this without too many pained memories. Is that a rhetorical question?"

"I'm just curious," he said. "You learn a lot about a man when he's faced with a tough decision. So what would you do, if you discovered this wasn't really your land?"

What a peculiar evening this was turning out to be. I'd started a topic that Smith seemed unable to leave. What the hell. The cabin wasn't something I had invested much money in, or even all that much time. I knew a man once who lived on a houseboat and who always said he could watch it sink and then go on and live somewhere else. And old Thoreau again, railing against possessing land, houses, furnishings: *Things are in the saddle, and they ride mankind.*

But what would I do if someone tried to take what I had? There is a powerful instinct to defend the cave, to fight against the intruder. And then, for no clear reason, I thought about the woman on the rock. "Smith, why are you focusing on this? Do you know something I don't?"

"I'm sure they's a hell of a lot I know that you don't. I don't know nothing about your land, though."

"OK," I said slowly, thinking my way through the answer, "if the Native Americans who once lived here wanted my land back, I'd work something out with them. I'd like to keep some of it, particularly the cabin, and I wouldn't want them building a casino next door to me, but I'd work out an agreement."

"Be easier to just kill them, though, wouldn't it?" he said with a sudden savage vehemence.

I stared at him in the light of the kerosene lantern. "And where the hell did that come from?"

He rocked for a moment, then said, "Well, that's the way you've been handling 'em for the past three hundred years, you white folks."

"Like me and Joseph Smith?"

Jeremiah nodded. "He is an ancestor of mine, that's the truth. And I'm white, probably Irish and Scotch stock. But my wife, Rebecca, was Abenaki, or at least mostly so."

I didn't say anything. I couldn't think of anything to say.

"She's been dead twenty years now," he said. "One hell of a good woman." He sipped his wine.

"All right," I said. "But tell me about what brought you out here to begin with. Tell me about your grandson."

Smith had his face turned toward me, but I had the sense he wasn't looking at me, just looking back into the past. "He was raised by Susan, our only child. See, a friend of Susan's got pregnant and there wasn't any question of an abortion. The girl left the baby over at Susan's place, that was when she was at Vermont College in Montpelier, and just vanished. Boy was two weeks old. They never did find the mother, and couldn't even find her family. She was one of those kids, just passing through, you know? The state was full of 'em back then. So Susan got adoption papers, named him Jerry, after me, and raised him. We all thought of him as ours."

"Does he know he was adopted?" I said.

"I expect. I've never discussed it with him, but probably Susan did."

"And where's she?"

"She died of breast cancer two years ago," he said, his voice blurred. "Seems they's an epidemic of it in this state. I think it's got something to do with those injections they give the cows, gets that stuff into the water, the runoff from the dairy farms."

"What about the boy's father?"

Smith stared at the floor for a long moment, then said, "Dunno. Susan never married and we never did see his birth mother again to ask her. This was thirty years ago, understand. For all I know, the boy's daddy might have been a soldier and died overseas. Country's been in enough wars in that time. Or maybe she just didn't know who it was, if you know what I mean. Things was different then."

It wasn't quite my time—I would have been a kid myself when the boy was born—but I remembered enough to nod.

Smith seemed lost in a reverie. "You know, the white people here didn't much like Indians back then, either. Rebecca's family and a lot of her kin up near Swanton mostly passed for white. Back in the 1930s in Vermont they tried to sterilize all the Abenaki. Before that, they shot 'em, mostly because some Abenaki were partners with the French during the War of 1812. So they got good at hiding. But they've always been here."

"Your bumper sticker," I said.

He nodded. "Yeah. State says the Abenaki don't exist. Official verdict of the Vermont Supreme Court in 1993, and they read the decision in front of a couple dozen Vermont Abenaki who were standing there waiting to hear what the government was gonna do. The court said they were all killed off or sterilized and because of the 'weight of history' for all practical purposes they had no rights to land and legally no longer existed. But they was always here, and they still are."

"I wonder if I saw one today," I said.

Smith blinked at me. "Pardon?"

OK, I'd started it. I'd climbed into the canoe spinning down this crazy conversational river, so I might as well put my oar in. I said, "I met a woman, dressed in buckskin, sitting on a stone in the forest when I was coming back from looking for the guy who shot at you."

"This that Sylvia? Where is she now?"

"That's the strange part. I happened onto her, talked to her for a couple of minutes, took my eyes off her, and she was just gone."

Smith nodded as if I'd just described a perfectly ordinary everyday event. He gave me a mirthless smile. "You notice if this Sylvia had real big eyes?" he said.

"Yes, I noticed that. Her face wasn't what you would call pretty, exactly, but overall she had a kind of grace, a kind of bearing that made her beautiful. I'd guess she was around twenty, maybe twenty-five, but it was hard to tell."

"*Nolka Alnôbak,*" he said. "No, don't ask me about it. It's an Indian word from these parts. We'll talk about it another time." He glanced out the dark window as if he expected to see somebody looking in. The windowpane was black and only reflected the light in the room back at us.

"I don't know what she was doing here," I said. "But somehow I don't think she had anything to do with what happened to us. She told me she heard the gunshots but didn't see the shooter."

"She talked to you." It was a statement, but implied a question, and he said it in a tone tinged with wonder.

"A little. I noticed she had an odd way of talking, not an accent, but . . . odd."

"Better to talk about it some other time or in some other place," he said, glancing toward the window again. "Or not to talk of it at all."

"All right," I said.

"So!" Smith said, leaning forward in his chair, his tone of voice and posture indicating I'd passed some sort of test. "Considering what somebody done to my truck and tried to do to me, you made up your mind yet? You gonna work for me? How about five thousand dollars as a starter, to give me two weeks of your time?"

Five thousand dollars. That was a fraction of what John Lincoln and I had charged for a day's work back in Atlanta. It was a different economy there, though, and we had only worked for corporations. "Go where the money is," Lincoln often said. The companies have the money, and would easily pay well for good and discreet work.

But five thousand dollars was a lot to Jeremiah Smith. I could tell by the weight he gave the words. And I was well and truly irritated that someone had the nerve to come onto the land that I called mine and destroy his property and shoot at the man.

I was already more than halfway persuaded, and Smith's expression told me he was reading me well. Just to keep him from getting too damn sure of himself, though, I said, "Let me sleep on it. I'll get back to you tomorrow. You sure you don't want to call the police?"

"Hell, no, they'd just make things worse. I want you on this one."

I stood up. "Tomorrow. I'll let you know then."

He wasn't satisfied but left it at that, and a few minutes later I put him into the Jeep, drove him into town, and dropped him off at Charlie-O's bar on Main Street.

If I'd known that was the last time I would see him alive, I might have had a few more questions to ask him.

5

Julio's downtown is a no-nonsense diner: no Formica tops, no mounted deer heads, and when it's your birthday you can order and pay for the special of the day, but no one is going to sing to you. The tables are blond oak, the heavy chairs the same. The china is as thick and substantial as the plates in the better class of prison used to be before the privatization insanity. A coffee cup holds twelve honest ounces and you pay for only the first fill. Julio's opens at six-thirty sharp. I was there at six-twenty, and Lucille let me in anyway.

"Don't think I've ever seen you here before noon." she said. "Breakfast?"

"I'm supposed to meet someone first." I had brought a newspaper, and I flopped it down onto the bar and sidelegged onto a stool. "Coffee would be welcome, though."

"Here you go."

One thing I missed about Atlanta: there the waitresses have a pet name for you the first time they see you. *Freshen your coffee up, Sugar? Want a li'l more pie, Honey?* Lucille, like the tables and the chairs and the plates, had no air of nonsense about her.

I pretended to scan the front page of the paper. It had taken me three calls to learn what Caleb Benson looked like and where and when he was likely to have breakfast. I wasn't about to start anything, but I wanted a look at the man Smith thought was going to kill his grandson.

At six-forty he came in with one other man. Benson proved easy to spot. He stood six-two with the shoulders of a lumberjack. I guessed he carried maybe 210 pounds, and he carried it well. Jeans, brown cowboy boots, a flannel shirt in a green-and-black plaid. He carried a folded-up orange *Financial Times* in his right hand as if it were a machete. The man with him was forty-something, dark hair, clean shaven, dressed in new jeans and a custom-made white cotton shirt with a thin blue stripe. He had the aura of an academic and the swagger of a businessman who kept in shape.

Benson apparently had a regular booth, given the way they went right to it and Julio himself came out to take their order.

I jerked my head at Lucille. "I'm giving up on my appointment," I told her. "I'll just take my coffee back there to a table where I can spread out my paper. If you could do me two eggs over easy, hash browns, and a double order of wheat toast, I'd be a happy man."

"You got it," she said.

Enough early customers had seeped in so that I was not particularly conspicuous. I meandered back, sipping my coffee, looking down at my folded paper, until I got to a table for two not so far from Benson's booth. I tossed the paper down and pulled out a chair. Then I spread the paper out and began to read. The president said we needed to tough it out a little longer in Iraq and Afghanistan. A study group was trying to discover why bees were dying. It had begun a couple of years before. It is to bees what the fundamentalist Christians think the Rapture will be to them: whole colonies of bees vanish overnight. If any are left in the hive, they are vitiated and weak and guarding a dwindled queen.

Someone once estimated that if the honeybee, which pollinates the majority of the foods we eat, ever goes extinct, humankind will follow in four years.

I turned the page just as Lucille brought my breakfast. While I ate and appeared to read, I was eavesdropping, with difficulty. Benson and his guest did not speak loudly or boisterously. Benson was saying in a calm voice, "But I have to be a hundred percent sure, Frank, that all that stuff is dead. Not ninety-nine. You need to think this through again."

"I've got everything covered," Frank said in a near whisper. "We clean it up, we take it as a loss. We don't want to try this again, even if they're certain it'll make a fortune. There's way too much goddamn risk."

"Do what you can on your end," Benson said. "And I'll wrap it up on mine."

Frank got up and walked out without another word, just as Benson got his breakfast. Benson ate quietly while he read his copy of the *Financial Times*. I finished my food and got a refill on the coffee. The cat in *Mutts* was playing with his little pink sock. The first word in the Jumble puzzle turned out to be *toque*, which gave me a hard time. And then Benson cleared his throat loudly, and when I looked up he crooked a finger at me.

There is a time and a place for machismo. Julio's at a little past seven in the morning is not it. I pushed back my chair and walked over to Benson. "Sit down, please," he said.

I sat on the empty bench opposite him.

"I assume you wanted to see me, Mr. Tyler," Benson said. "Here I am."

I frowned. "I was having my breakfast and reading the paper. I don't know you. I've never met you, never seen you before this morning. Why should I give a damn about you, mister?"

"What did old Jeremiah Smith tell you last night?" Benson asked.

He was good. He had a high forehead, dark hair crinkling up from it in a widow's peak. I couldn't read his eyes, nor quite name their color: dark, nearly black, but whether blue or an unusual dark gray, I couldn't say. His face was not a handsome one, but it held weight and authority. You saw faces like that on old Roman sculptures. And he exuded something, a sense of contained power. Sitting opposite him was a bit like having a picnic on the shoulder of Mount St. Helens.

"Jeremiah's a friend of mine," I said. "He helps me drink my wine."

"I am sure you have some mighty fine wine," Benson said without cracking a smile. "Jeremiah Smith has some odd ideas about me, Mr. Tyler. I trust you have the sense to question anything a prospective client might say to you. Please rest assured that I have no ill-will against the old man. If he has hired you—"

I laughed. "You look as if you know a few things, or ought to. Feel free to check and see what sort of fees Lincoln and Tyler charged, and what sort of clients we took on."

"It was a small fortune," he said. "A corporate clientele. And very discreet service. Mostly you guys did international industrial espionage or recovery of stolen goods."

I nodded. "And so you will know that I sold out and retired."

"I heard you got a cabin outside of town. Why live so poorly when you musta cashed out well?"

"I always loved Thoreau," I said. "Wouldn't want to die without having tried a simple life."

"For how long?"

I shrugged. "I don't know. So far it's surprisingly fulfilling."

He nodded. We nodded at each other. It began to feel like a Japanese tea ceremony. To break the stretching silence, I finally said, "Now if I may ask an equally personal question, who the hell are you?"

"Don't insult my intelligence, Mr. Tyler."

I grinned. "All right, Mr. Benson, I will not. Jeremiah implied you were a dangerous man whose activities ought to be looked into. He more than hinted that you could have inconvenient people removed."

Benson spread his hands. "Did he tell you how many people I employ? How much of the area's economy depends directly upon me or upon one of my companies? I doubt that very much. I am a businessman, not a murderer, Mr. Tyler. Any money-making activity takes a small toll on the environment. My businesses do. But we operate within the letter of the law. We harvest trees, true, but we replant when we do. We produce materials that are toxic, but we detoxify them or dispose of them so they are no threat. The simple truth, Mr. Tyler, is that people like Smith despise me because they think I am despoiling their world, changing it for the worse. But whether I am here or not, the world will change. It is change they fear, not me."

"I'll tell him so," I said. "Now, if you'll excuse me, I have an appointment."

Benson nodded, and looked back down at his *Financial Times*, dismissing me. I got up, dropped a couple of dollars on my table as I walked by it, then went up front to where Lucille was working the register. "He's paid for yours," she said, nodding back toward the booth.

"No he hasn't," I said, handing her one of the bills I had received from Smith. "He's just given you an extra tip, that's all."

She didn't argue. I took my change and walked out into the clear-aired morning.

◆

I could have gone straight from Julio's to Smith's place. He'd given me the address the night before, a trailer park outside Northfield, when I was driving him in to the bar. I should probably have done that, but I felt the need to think about things for a while. And I told myself that it could wait.

So I drove back out of town, out to the logging road, and as far up it as I could, just past the blackened spot where the truck had burned. The newspaper said it would be another unseasonably warm day, but then an arctic blast was due out of Canada in a day or two.

To be on the safe side I stopped at one of three woodpiles and got an armload of firewood. Toted it to the back of the cabin and dumped it in the sheltered lee near the plywood trapdoor. Went back down for another armload, and another. Kept at it for three or four loads past what felt necessary, until my lungs were heaving and my shoulders aching. Then, feeling righteous, I went back into my cabin and checked my phone. There are solar panels on the roof that charge a 12-volt marine battery. The marine battery provides enough power to keep my cell phone charged through a little Radio Shack 12-volt-to-110-volt inverter, and to run the radio when I decide to turn it on, which is pretty much never.

I built a fire and took out my book. Somehow something would be settled, or my subconscious would settle it. It is a kind of faith I have.

A solitary lunch, a solitary dinner. Night came on, and I stepped outside to see what the air tasted like. It was a thick darkness. Around the cabin, the forest was that kind of deep, deep black that comes with a heavy overcast on a winter night. No stars, no moon, and out here in the mountains, not even the lights of a nearby city. I walked down to the Jeep, more by instinct than vision, wanting to be out just to keep my ears open. Absurdly, I had the feeling that there were eyes in that darkness.

I reached the Jeep, a barely discernible block in the gloom. The wind was getting cold. I stood there breathing it in for ten minutes or so. Nothing, no sound. Somehow I did not relish the climb back up to the cabin through the darkness, so I opened the Jeep and found the small kerosene railroad lamp that I kept there for emergencies or the darkest of nights. I lit it and in its ruddy glow headed back toward the cabin, the swinging light causing shadows to move and flicker as if the trees were dancing.

Unexpectedly, I smelled wood smoke billowing down the hillside. When I had left, the fire had burned down to a bed of red embers. I broke into a faster step, following the trail through the snow that Jeremiah had stamped out the previous day, and my heart beat fast, apprehensive that I had done something spectacularly stupid and that the cabin was on fire.

But it wasn't. It stood there square and solid as ever, and yellow light, lantern light, streamed out the windows. I knew damned well that I had extinguished the lantern inside before I left, to allow my eyes to accustom themselves to the gloom.

I flipped up the globe on the railroad lamp I was carrying and blew out the wick: the forest expanded around me in the sudden blackness as if the land had exhaled.

Fifty feet to my right I heard a mournful hoot as an owl surveyed the slim pickings of a winter forest where snow protected the burrows of the field mice. I took careful steps, watching the windows closely for signs of movement within the cabin, but also scanning the area around me for any evidence of an ambush. If the light in the cabin was bait, I didn't intend to walk into the trap. I wrapped one hand around the Police Special in my pocket. It had been there all day, ever since I had decided to have breakfast at Julio's.

I saw through the front window a flicker of motion: somebody was sitting in one of the rocking chairs, moving gently back and forth. My space was being violated. With a self-righteous sense of indignation, I marched up to the door and threw it open.

The woman I'd seen the day before—Sylvia—was sitting in the straight-backed rocker. She smiled at me, a juice glass full of my wine in her hand. "Welcome back from the world of the forest spirits," she said, raising the glass in a salute. Her smile was warm and friendly, her speech still careful and precise. She was wearing the same tight-fitting buckskin pants, shirt, and moccasins.

"What are you doing here?" I asked, relaxing my hold on the pistol in my pocket.

"You had a request," she said simply. "You wanted to know what to do with the rest of your life."

That threw me. To hide my confusion, I poured myself a glass of wine, noting that she had stoked the stove and trimmed the lantern, adjusting the wick so it gave a clear, smokeless light. I sat in the other rocker. "I think you have the wrong guy."

"This is excellent wine. A good drug to keep a populace docile." She smiled as if we had just shared a private joke and took another delicate sip.

"Beats nicotine," I said. "So, for the sake of argument, what would you recommend I do with my life?"

"You could save the creatures of the world," she said, face and voice utterly serious.

I stared at her. "Are you a missionary? From some religious group?"

"It is not necessarily a religious effort, is it? You don't consider yourself very religious, yet you try to save people."

"I've tried now and again," I said, and drank half my wine. "I've also hurt people, some very badly."

"Killed some?"

"Yes."

"But always to save others. The weak who cannot help themselves."

"The rich weak," I corrected, wondering what the pitch was and when it was going to come. Join us, my brother. Come to our compound in beautiful Belize. Have a cup of Kool-Aid.

She looked at the light through her wine, speculatively. "Do you think the world is dying?"

The question startled me into momentary honesty: "It seems like it. That's why I came here from Atlanta."

"Are people evil?" she asked. "Essentially, I mean. Are most humans evil?"

"There are times I think so." God, I hadn't had a conversation like this since my disastrous freshman year in college.

"Could you be persuaded otherwise? That most humans are essentially decent and kind, but their actions may become evil because they lack understanding?"

"I've never thought about it."

"But you have." She looked at me with her odd, large eyes. "What do you think of the earliest people who lived here? That they were savages, primitives? That they ran around scalping each other? Always fighting wars, half-starved most of the time? That is what your schools teach you, isn't it?"

"Something like that."

"There were times when the people of old broke the Law. The Law of Nature, I mean. Such people have no idea of the right, the good, the polite thing to do."

I couldn't help chuckling. "The polite thing to do is not to come into a stranger's house and help yourself to his wine."

"No, in certain contexts it is very good manners to do so, particularly if the wine is out where anyone can see, an open invitation. And a friendly glass of wine is not much in repayment for my answering the question you asked at the turning of the year, when you scattered your friend's ashes over a pile of stones."

"You were there? You saw that?"

"No. Squirrel told me."

"Who's that?" I remembered then: a gray critter head-down, high in a tree, chattering. "Wait—you don't mean a real squirrel, do you? An animal?"

She didn't answer me. Just looked at me with those doe eyes.

"Look," I said, "I realize your people might believe—why are you laughing?"

"You still think I am an Abenaki. I am not. I am not even a Native American. My people were here when the Abenaki arrived. Don't ask me the tribe, for it is not a tribe. And I could not pronounce our name with these lips." She gave me a gaze of such placid confidence that I wanted to hug her.

But I channeled the feeling into irony. "So a squirrel told you I buried a friend and said some words. What else do you hear from your squirrel friend?"

She looked down at the rug. "That Jeremiah Smith died today, just twenty minutes ago, outside of Northfield. He was walking because he did not have a truck. A car struck him, and he died instantly."

"What!"

"It was a car with license plates a different color from those of Vermont. Squirrel does not see colors the same as you, so I cannot describe it, and of course Squirrel does not read, does not know letters and numbers. But it was a dark car, and it came fast and swerved on purpose to hit the old man."

"A squirrel told you this?"

"Not a squirrel. Squirrel. A squirrel is an individual animal. Squirrel is . . . like the spirit of all of the individual creatures, the great reality that shapes them and gives them purpose and sees through all their eyes and hears through all their ears."

"I hope Squirrel is wrong," I said. "Because you've been here for more than twenty minutes. And if Jeremiah is dead and the police come asking me, and it turns out that he was killed as you say—well, they won't believe that the spirit of a squirrel tipped you off."

"I know," she said. "They would think that I heard by telephone or radio. But I do not own any electronic devices."

"Or they'd think you were involved with the killing," I said. "That you were in on it."

"Believe that if you must," she said. "But Jeremiah believed in you and trusted you. He knew about me and my people. I am not worried about the police. They could not find me. But let me warn you not to speak to anyone about what I have told you tonight. If you do, I will never return to you again."

"And my life would get back to normal," I said. "How could I face that?"

"You can answer that," she said. "I cannot." Carefully she set her empty wine glass down on the floor, bending over from the waist in a curiously lithe movement. Without glancing back at me, she turned and walked to the door, pushed it open, and stepped through into the black, starless night. Watching her leave, I was struck by how totally female she was, and how hard I'd been trying to ignore it while she'd sat with me in my cabin.

"Hey," I said. "Wait. Come back."

I opened the door onto darkness. No sound, not even the wind. No crunch of footsteps on crusted snow. She had faded into the night. I finished the last gulp of my wine and stood there, wondering just what the hell had happened, until I started to shiver. Then I went back inside and made sure my cell phone was charged before checking the recently called numbers.

6

I pulled up the last number Smith had dialed when he'd had my phone, after his gas tank exploded.

After two rings, a man's rough voice said, "Yeah?"

"Jeremiah Smith there?" I said, keeping my voice casual, as if I were asking for an old friend.

After a pause, the same voice asked, "Who's this?"

"Oakley Tyler. He visited me yesterday. I'm trying to get in touch with him about something he asked me. Who's this?"

"This is Bill—wait a minute, you called me. You don't know?"

"Oh yeah, guy with the tow truck, right?"

He snorted. "Yeah, that's me." He paused for a moment, then said in a flat tone, "Smith's dead."

I shivered as a wave of cold moved through my body. "When?"

"Half hour ago, maybe a little more. I just got off the phone with the chief."

"Chief of police?"

"Yeah. I was apparently the last guy saw him alive. He came in to hear about the damage to his truck. He stayed for dinner here, and then was gonna hitchhike to Montpelier to see his grandson."

"Hitchhike?"

"Lotsa people do. In these parts, anyway." His voice had a defensive scorn, as if my question had betrayed a flatlander's ignorant elitism.

"How did Smith die?"

"Hit-and-run."

"Any witnesses?"

"None they can find, but maybe tomorrow after it's in the paper somebody will turn up." A phlegmy sigh seemed to signal Bill Grinder's decision to stop making me reach for every bit of information with a pair of tweezers. "OK, here's how it was. He was walking north on Route Twelve, about a mile outside of town, where he was hit. Not long after that, the cops say, another driver saw his body on the side of the road and dialed nine-one-one on their cell. He was dead when they called, though. The driver checked."

"How'd the police get a reading on time of death?"

"From me, I guess. Like I told them, Jeremiah left here during the first commercial after the seven-thirty news started on Fox, so it was probably seven thirty-five or close to it. The car found him at ten minutes to eight. He'd walked about a mile, which takes around fifteen minutes. Don't take rocket science." He was getting tired of talking, I could tell. Or just resentful.

"Was the driver that found him local or out-of-state?"

"How the hell should I know? Wait, no, it was local, had to be, because it was that girl works at the drugstore in town, it'd closed at seven and she was on her way home." He paused for a moment. "Smith said you was some kind of cop?"

"Private. He came to see me about a problem."

"So whyn't you call the cops and ask them?"

"Sorry, Bill. Just an old habit. I apologize for taking up your time."

I heard the volume of a TV set in the background being turned up, had a vision of him sitting with a remote in his hand. And then there was a click and the line was dead: he'd hung up.

So let the police handle it. Too bad I didn't get back to Smith, but it's out of my hands. Now he'd never be able to answer my questions about why Caleb Benson had reacted to me the way he had in the restaurant, about how he had known of Smith's visit to my cabin, about why Smith was so concerned about his grandson. Smith was beyond telling me now. But I still had just over ninety dollars of his money in my wallet. I wondered if maybe Mr. Benson might need something more to worry about than his payroll or EPA regulations. Decided to give him something to worry about.

Before tilting at his windmills, Don Quixote armed himself with a rusty lance. I picked up the gun and put it back into my jacket pocket, slipped the cell phone into the other pocket, and went out the door and into the night.

◆

Walking carefully in the dark, I followed the rutted trail of my own footsteps down to the Jeep. Cold air cut my nose and made my eyes water. Twice I called for Sylvia, but heard no sound of her, saw no sign. At the Jeep I paused and called her name again. Still no reply. I got into the Jeep, started it, flipped on the high beams, and drove down the last of the logging trail and out onto the town-maintained road. It was snowing again, not hard but steady, and the night flaked into what looked like volcanic ash in the twin headlight beams.

I drove two miles north, farther than she could have walked in that time, and then turned around and went back four miles south. No sign of her. If she'd had a vehicle parked nearby, it must have been far enough down the road that I didn't hear her start it, but close enough that she could get to it and get out of the area before I had finished my phone conversation with Grinder and come looking.

But it didn't make sense that anybody could make it down a rocky, hilly, twisting trail at a dead run in total darkness. Maybe she was still hiding back there in the forest, or maybe somebody picked her up. Maybe a coconspirator with a shot-gun microphone and a cell phone or radio, and boots bigger than size ten.

Heading toward town, I thought of Jeremiah Smith, and a slow anger washed over me. The plastic steering wheel creaked, protesting my painful grip on it, and I exhaled and let go, feel-ing the blood return to my fingers. The old man who'd been so alive yesterday afternoon, who'd come to get my help to save another life, was dead.

He was about John Lincoln's age.

Snow swirled and danced ahead of me. Curtains of it brushed the road. I drove without really noticing much of anything until up ahead I saw a rusty sign with a bad case of the quaints and the cutesies: YE QUALITY MECHANIC. Grind-er's red tow truck was tucked beside it, in front of a house that looked like it hadn't been painted in a decade or more. The blue light of television leaked out of one window, like a strange species of radioactive gas, and I guessed that was where Grinder lived. A mile north of that I came to the scene of the hit-and-run.

The investigation had not yet wound down. An empty Ver-mont State Police car with its engine running and headlights on hummed on the gravel shoulder of the road behind a Northfield Police car, its engine also chugging. Both cars sent ragged gusts of exhaust into the night. In my headlights the gray vapor ascended through the snow like ghosts seeking heaven.

Two men sat in the Northfield car. I pulled up behind them and was about halfway out the door when both of the cruiser's front doors flew open and the cop on the driver's side emerged and said, "Step out of the vehicle." The passenger cop wore a state trooper hat and a cold expression, and in his hand a pistol pointed in my general direction.

I finished my climb out of the car and put both my hands at my sides, where they could see them.

The Northfield patrolman walked up to me. He looked to me the more competent of the two, a muscular man in his early thirties with close-cropped blond sideburns showing under the edge of his cap. He walked ramrod straight; his face was wide with large pale-green eyes and a long nose that looked like it had been broken once. Unlike his buddy, he had an air of authority that did not need a gun to front for it. He stopped just in front of me and said, "Help you with something?"

"Bill Grinder tells me Jeremiah Smith was hit and killed along in here."

The patrolman's face did not change expression. "And who are you, sir?"

Nice to know I rated a "sir." I told him my name and added, "I live on the other side of town, near the Roxbury line."

"You the PI? Moved here from Atlanta?" I caught the faintest whiff of derision in the last word, a phony Southern drawl. They never get that right. And they think we use "y'all" as a singular pronoun.

"That's right," I said.

Contrary to what you see on TV, most cops hate PIs. They figure we make more money, have longer and more frequent vacations, and don't have to live by all the rules. They're wrong, but with reasons. One is there are a lot of incompetent PIs in the world, so most cops know by heart a dozen or more stories of investigations around the country that some private heat screwed up. Some of them spin yarns about brother cops getting seriously killed because a PI stuck his nose in where it did not belong.

"Mr. Tyler, I need to see your ID." The kid kept his tone flatly neutral, and my appreciation of his ability ratcheted up by maybe one notch. If I knew of some rotten PIs, I knew of even more small-town cops that had no grasp of professional conduct.

I pulled out my Vermont driver's license and handed it to him. Snow blew past so cold that it burned my cheek when it hit.

Holding his flashlight up beside his left ear, the cop looked over the license, then turned the beam on me. "You carrying?"

"I am."

"Where's the weapon?"

"My right-hand jacket pocket."

"Take it out slowly and give it to me, handle-first."

So maybe he wasn't as professional as I'd thought. But I complied, meanwhile telling him, "Word I got was that I didn't need a concealed-carry permit in Vermont. I still have a valid one for Georgia." I handed him the weapon.

He offered no comment on what I understood about gun laws in Vermont. In the glare of his flashlight he inspected the gun, then broke the cylinder and spun it. He sniffed the barrel, then let his arm drop, pointing the weapon at the ground. "Got any others?"

"No handguns on me or in the Jeep. That's it. I have a shotgun in my cabin."

The state cop seemed to be antsy. He came around the cruiser holding his sidearm in both hands, barrel aimed just above my car. "What'cha got, Jess?"

"PI. Got a piece, but he's legal. I've heard about him."

The trooper made a flicking gesture with the barrel of his gun. He was starting to make me nervous, to make me wonder if he'd learned firearm technique from a qualified instructor or from watching Arnold and Bruce and Nick on Netflix DVDs. "What you figure you need a weapon for?"

"Would you please not aim so close to my head?"

"Holster it," Jess told his state trooper friend.

After a five-second pause, the ten-year-old's *I don't hafta if I don't wanna*, the state cop decided he wanted to and put his sidearm away. Relaxing a little, I gave him as much as he needed to know: "I had the piece with me because yesterday Jeremiah Smith came to see me at my place. While he was there somebody torched his truck, and when we went to look at the damage, someone took a shot at us."

"Why did they do that?"

"I don't know. Either he didn't like Smith or he didn't like me. I can't imagine any scenario where the latter would be the case, so I'm guessing it was someone with a grudge against Smith."

It was too far to push on a cold, snowy night. Jess had not handed my license back to me. He passed it to the trooper and said, "Larry, do me a favor and run him for us." In the back glow from the flashlight I saw him smile. "Sorry for this, but you know if we pig-ignorant cops don't do it by the book, we get our asses chewed."

Larry got my license plate number, walked back to his cruiser, and climbed in. Jess hefted my gun thoughtfully in his right hand. "Before he gets back, tell me what's your interest here."

"Just what I told you. Somebody fired at us yesterday, actually grazed Smith's ear, and now he's dead." I was starting to shiver. Jess didn't seem to be bothered by the wind.

"Who you working for?"

"Nobody's paying me," I said truthfully.

"You didn't report the shooting. That's a crime in itself."

"I didn't get hit. Smith was the injured party, and he decided it was a hunting accident."

"Yeah. You know I could toss your ass in jail. I could have your PI license pulled."

"You could, but I'm not working at it any longer. I retired when my partner died."

"Jim Lincoln."

"John. Heart attack."

"OK," the cop said, handing me my weapon back. I guessed that he'd known John's first name all along and that it had been a little test. What the hell, it didn't cost a thing. "You see the shooter? Able to tell us anything about him?"

"Didn't see him. From tracks I saw near the Dog River, he wears size eleven or twelve boots. Big guy, I'd say."

Larry climbed out of the State Police cruiser and came back with my driver's license. He handed it to me and growled to Jess, "He's clean. And the car."

"Know anything about what happened here, Mr. Tyler?" asked Jess, putting a little extra twist on the "Mister."

"Heard from Grinder it was a hit-and-run."

"That all?"

"That's it. I thought I'd stop and see if I could help."

He slapped the door of my jeep. "Good to see a citizen with that kind of social conscience. Thank you for stopping, sir. Good evening."

My nose was freezing, and the snow was coming down harder. "No charge for the offer of help. Call it professional courtesy. And by the way, did the woman who found Smith have out-of-state plates on her car?"

Larry bulled forward. "Damned odd question. What are you getting at?"

"Just curious."

Jess elbowed in front of Larry. "Mr. Tyler, you realize we can't answer a civilian's questions on this matter."

"All right."

He hesitated, but then added, "If you hear anything we ought to know, or if you come across anything funny, you'll notify us."

It wasn't a question.

"I'd like to see the whole thing resolved," I said carefully.

Neither cop replied. Both of them walked back to their cars, over at least an inch of fresh snowfall. I slipped the gun back into my pocket, got in the Jeep, rolled the window up, and turned around. I drove back through near-blinding snow to Bill Grinder's house, thinking resentfully that when old Don Quixote shambled off on his bony nag to pursue the elusive windmill, at least he did so in sunny Spain.

7

Bill Grinder grudgingly let me in. His living room looked as if it had been decorated by a taxidermist with delusions of grandeur. Deer heads, a moose head, a bobcat, and a baby bear stared at me with glass eyes. A flat high-definition TV screen not quite as large as a billboard occupied most of the wall beside the front door, and in its light spill I saw a sagging sofa and a cracked recliner, with small tables beside each of them cluttered with stuffed weasels, a family of rabbits, and a skunk. I imagined that I could smell it, but the sour air was really just full of the odors of dust, old wood, and moldy hides.

Grinder half-sat, half-lay in the recliner. Lucy, an obese woman of fifty—I assumed she was his wife, but Grinder had just introduced her with "This's Lucy"—was on the far end of the couch, wrapped in a flower-patterned house dress and munching stolidly on popcorn. They had been watching a show about a snotty young guy who faked being a psychic and showed up the ordinary cops. They didn't look away from the screen as I talked to them, but Grinder, at least, answered my questions.

"The woman that found him? Her name's Tammy, Tammy Ehrlman. Lives in Riverton. Her old man is—what is he, Lucy?"

"Town selectman," Lucy said. "Tammy's a good girl."

"Is she in the phone book?"

He flipped a hand toward an end table. A Princess phone, a real antique of the sort that shows up on eBay, sat atop a dog-eared and oil-stained local telephone directory. I opened it and squinted in the light of the TV until I found a listing for Ehrl-man. I took out my cell phone and dialed it. A man answered.

"Is Tammy there?" I asked.

"Who's calling?" His tone sounded more bored than protective.

"My name is Oakley Tyler. I was a friend of Jeremiah Smith's."

A pause, then, "Tammy can't come to the phone, Mr. Tyler. She's sedated. Got all shook up finding him there, so she took a sleeping pill and went to bed. She needs to sleep it off."

"Can you tell me if she was driving her own car when she found Mr. Smith?"

"She was."

"Does it have Vermont plates?"

"What? Sure. And the tag's current."

"Does anyone in the household have out-of-state plates?"

"What?" he asked again. "No. Why?"

"I'm trying to locate a possible witness," I said.

"Well, I think you'd need more to go on than that," he said. "Look, I don't know of anybody around here who drives a car with out-of-state plates, OK? If you want to talk to Tammy, she'll be at work in the morning."

He hung up on me. Before I could put my phone back in my pocket, Lucy's moon face turned toward me, her eyes wide. "What about out-of-state license plates?"

"I had a lead that a car seen near the site of the accident had out-of-state plates."

"Can't be anybody from here. You live here, you got to get Vermont plates." She creased her forehead. "I don't get out much. Bill, you seen anybody driving around town with out-of-state plates?"

"Shit, no," he said. The show broke for a commercial. Grinder frowned at Lucy and said, "You got to talk all the damn time? Whyn't you haul your ass back up the street and watch your own damn TV?"

She gave him an indignant look. "You invited me over! I made dinner for you and Jeremiah."

"And we ate it, didn't we? You want a medal?"

"I want you to answer this man's question," she said. "Stop stalling, Bill. Anybody around here driving with out-of-state plates?"

He glared at her, but he said, "I see 'em all the time. People coming up for the skiing, or the fall colors. Go hiking in the summer." He turned to me. "Guess you ain't figured out that this is kind of a tourist town. Thought you was a big famous detective. How about you, Tyler? You got out-of-state plates on that Jeep of yours?"

"No. Bought the vehicle at the dealer in Barre, just outside Montpelier."

He snorted. "We get flatlanders comin' in here, drivin' up property prices and taxes, and they all think they're smarter than us Vermonters."

"And you think I'm one?"

"Shit." The show was back on. He turned back toward the TV. "Jeremiah was my friend," he said.

I didn't know where I stood with these two. I said, "I'll go in a minute. First, though, can you tell me anything about Jeremiah's grandson?"

Lucy said, "I know who he is, know him to see. He's a reporter. He lives in Montpelier." She giggled and jerked her chins toward Bill. "He don't like him, 'cause the boy's a liberal!"

I raised my eyebrows.

"No, it's true," she said. "He's always writing about how we ought to save the owls—"

"Shit," Grinder commented.

"—and all that stuff. He wants to make people stop cutting trees on their own land."

Bill turned a scowling face to me. "That boy wants the damn government in everybody's business! Let him have his way, half the damn state'd be unemployed."

"Where does he work?"

Lucy knew: "Writes for *This Week*, little local paper, comes out every Friday."

Bill grunted. "He spreads some of his crap around in magazines, too. *Vermont Life*. The *New Englander*. Liberal shit."

"Did he live with Jeremiah?"

Lucy didn't know, but Bill did: "Hell no. That old coot couldn't stand the boy for more than an hour at a time. No, Jeremiah lives—lived—in a house trailer just north of Northfield, but the boy has an apartment in Montpelier." Bill's face showed a quiet struggle of emotion, and then he said, "Hell, I don't wanna give you the wrong impression. They bickered and all, but you know, they was family. The boy, Jerry, he lived with his mom and Jeremiah for about four, five years when she was sick, but after she died Jerry wanted to move out on his own."

I stood to leave and hesitated. "Do either of you know a Native American woman named Sylvia?"

Grinder grunted. "Don't know any Injuns. Don't want to."

I persisted: "This one's young, late twenties, early thirties. Straight black hair, long, down to the middle of her back. She wears buckskins and moccasins."

"No, don't know her," Grinder said tightly. Lucy shook her head.

"Let me borrow your phone book one more time," I said. Montpelier had a good number of Smiths, including a fair number of J. Smiths. But Jerry had his own listing. I dialed his number on my cell phone and got an answering machine, but I didn't leave a message. I took out a small pocket notebook and wrote down his number and address.

On TV the smarmy young mock-psychic had just made a policeman look like a fool. Grinder and Lucy both laughed, he sounding as if he were drowning, she spraying a buckshot pattern of chewed popcorn. Neither of them seemed to mind my leaving.

◆

It seemed to me I owed Jerry Smith at least a visit and a talk, so I set off north on Route 12, a two-lane highway with a 50 MPH speed limit. It had been the main link between Montpelier and points south before the superhighway came through. I rode the tunnel of my high beams through the night. The road ahead was empty for the eleven miles of forests and fields to the state capital. I pushed the Jeep to sixty, but didn't dare to go faster than that, not with snow drifting across the road, not with possible black ice in my path.

It was past ten. Traffic in Montpelier was light, and I found the apartment house with no trouble. I pressed the buzzer under Jerry Smith's name, but got no answer. A young couple came up just as I was about to go back to my car, and the woman said, "Are you looking for Jerry?"

"I am," I said.

The man pointed toward the street. "You just missed him. Charlene and I saw him get into a car with some guys. They went tear-assing off south not a minute ago."

"He was drunk," Charlene said. "Took two of them to hold him up straight and get him into the car."

Something cold turned over in my stomach. I was already running toward the Jeep.

South took me directly back onto Route 12. I thought I might catch them if they hadn't turned off. I should have asked about the car, the make and model. Getting rusty. I pushed the Jeep hard, the needle nudging seventy.

And a few miles south of town, I had to find the brakes in a hurry. I thought I saw someone step out into my lane at the far reach of my headlights. The Jeep wanted to fishtail for a second, but I got it over onto the shoulder and came to a stop.

Deer. Two does, one in each lane, both of them staring at me. They twitched and quivered as I braked the Jeep to a halt, as if every instinct was telling them to get the hell out of there, but something was locking them in place.

And then I heard, as faint as a mosquito whine, a scream.

I opened the door and got out, and that broke the spell. The deer took off in unison, leaping over the shoulder, into the woods off to the left. I heard another scream from the right. From the darkness. I checked my gun in my jacket pocket, and followed the shoulder of the road to the source of the sounds of pain.

8

I hadn't seen it from the highway, but an abandoned road led downhill and into the dark forest. Twenty yards away from Route 12, I might have been dropped into the heart of pre-Columbian Vermont. The old road, probably a logging trail, bore the recent tracks of tires. Off to the right I caught a glint of metal. It was a dark Subaru four-wheel-drive station wagon, turned to face the highway, turned for a quick getaway. Vermont plates.

Through the trees ahead I spied a gleam of light, and I could hear the mutter and growl of men's voices. I missed the way somehow, and instead of coming out on a level with the three men in the clearing, I found myself peering over the edge of a steep drop. They were about six feet below me. A kerosene lantern dimly lit the scene. One man, a young one, stood with his back against a birch, his hands out of sight behind him. I guessed he was handcuffed around the trunk. The other two men were bulky shadows against the glare of the lantern.

One was saying, "We could kill you. We could do it in ways no one would ever discover. A little plutonium, a little dioxin, and you'd die of cancer in a few months. Or we could scratch you with a resistant strain of strep and in a week it'll eat the flesh off your bones. One of us could walk past you in the street, spray you with a mist carrying antibiotic-resistant pneumonia. We could make it look like stroke or a heart attack. You know that, don't you, kid?" His voice sounded familiar.

The young man cuffed or tied to the tree was leaning forward. He jerked his head, trying to throw his longish brown hair out of his eyes. He wore only blue jeans, standing barefoot in a few inches of snow. His stomach bore some angry pink welts, like insect bites that had become infected. The man talking to him was taller than the captive. I couldn't see much of him against the light, but he wore a heavy jacket, and he carried something in his hand, a gun I thought at first. But then he moved a little and I saw that it looked more like a TV remote than a weapon.

"You're making a huge mistake," the young man said.

"No. You made the mistake," the large man answered softly. He reached out and touched the device to his captive's stomach, and the boy's body convulsed, his eyes bulged, and a scream erupted from his stomach and came out his mouth.

"Don't kill him," the third man in the tableau said, his voice frightened, whiny. "I ain't here for any killing."

I began to edge to the left, where the land fell away, hunting for a spot where I could get into the clearing without causing a small avalanche of stone and snow. The man with the stun gun said in a bored voice, "I'm not going to kill him."

Maybe not. The kid had been hit with probably seventy-five thousand volts at a low amperage, so low that the shock doesn't kill or even scar. But the jolt hits you with blinding pain, far worse than being bludgeoned with a brick. There are places in the world, and too many of them here in the United States, where the police or the army get a lot of enjoyment applying these devices to the genitals of men, women, and teenagers.

I pulled back, losing sight of the clearing for half a minute, and worked my way around so I was on level ground. I stepped into the light to the left of the Taser-armed man. He was just about to apply it to the kid's fluttering stomach again. I said, "Step back slowly, drop the Taser, and turn around, or I'll shoot you where you stand."

"Jesus," the man said in a tired, irritated voice, like a plumber who had just discovered he had forgotten a wrench. "Who the hell are you?" He backed away, further into the shadow.

"I ask the questions," I said, suddenly and coldly aware that the man with the whiny voice was no longer in sight.

"You got him in your sights?" the heavy man asked.

"Got him."

Damn. Off in the trees somewhere. They must have heard me coming. I heard the distinctive ratchet of a pump-action rifle.

"So who the hell are you?" the older man asked me again, his voice sounding like there was a little smile on his lips.

"The guy who's betting he can get off one shot even if he's hit," I said. "And believe me, I'm good with this gun. But since your friend has a rifle, maybe I should just shoot you right now and even up the odds a little." I had dropped a flashlight into my side pocket; from the same pocket I produced my cell phone, flipped it open, and punched in 911. I stood with my thumb on the send button.

"Who are you calling?" the man asked. I couldn't quite place the accent. It was closest to the affected Boston accent that kids from other parts of the country pick up if they attend Harvard.

"Guess," I said. "They can figure out where cell calls are made from. If your friend doesn't make a good shot, the police will know exactly where I was when I called. How long do you think it'll take them to get here? How long do you think it'll take you and your buddy to replace the two front tires that I flattened?"

He didn't like that. His face tightened. "I don't much like guns," he said conversationally. "They make a mess. Nevertheless, hunting accidents are common. My friend is holding a standard-issue thirty-aught-six on you. Some years ago, the head of the FBI died in a hunting accident—"

"Bill Sullivan," I said. "Died in 1977. But nobody's going to buy that. Deer season is over."

His face became grave. "There are complications," he said with a sigh. "We seem to be at a standoff. What do you suggest?"

"Tell squeaky to come into the light, where I can see him. And you step forward, too."

I had been moving slowly back. Now I stood mostly in darkness. The man said, "We're just having a little business meeting here." It seemed an odd turn of phrase.

"Tell your boss that you hit some hard luck," I suggested. "This time, let's call it a draw."

"This time?"

"It might be different next time," I told him.

The guy off to the side whined, "I don't like this!"

"Shut up and do what I tell you," the man yelled back. "Keep your rifle on him. If I tell you to shoot, kill him."

"That's murder," the whiner said.

"He has a weapon. It would be self-defense. Just shut the fuck up and come on," the older man said.

The second man, the whiner, edged toward the light. He was holding his rifle at hip level. He hung just far enough back so I couldn't make out his features, but the lantern caught the muzzle of the rifle, its unwinking deadly black eye. It was easy to imagine that I could see right down the barrel to the neat pointed tip of the bullet. I glanced at the kid tied to the tree and saw that he was following all this with eager eyes. He was shivering, and I'd bet his feet were close to frostbite, but the scene in the clearing was fascinating him.

"We will back out of here," the man told me. "But I have to ask: Who are you?"

"Just a concerned citizen. I heard a scream from the road, called the cops, and came to see what was happening."

"What's your name?"

"Jim Thomas. Didn't I hear your voice in the diner, talking with Caleb Benson?"

"Never heard of him." He jerked a thumb. "You know this kid?"

"Never seen him before in my life."

"Come on, come on," the whiner said.

Then the tied-up kid surprised me. He jerked his head up. "Siren," he said.

We stood listening to silence, but it was easy to imagine that the wind in the trees was the distant wail of an approaching cruiser.

"Back out of here," I said. I edged around and side-kicked the kerosene lantern. It hit a tree, went out, leaving us in glimmering darkness, ruining the whiner's aim. "Get on out."

They blundered away. A few seconds later I heard the Subaru fire up. "Who were they? What were they torturing you for?" I asked the kid as I pulled the flashlight out of my pocket.

"I don't know who or why." He had been tied, not cuffed, with a good but quick-release knot. I got him loose. "My socks and shoes," he said, rubbing his wrists. "My shirt and jacket."

I found them in a heap and he got them on. "Just the two of them?" I asked.

He was shaking, hiccupping, probably from shock and relief. "Yeah."

"You're Jerry Smith."

He paused in the act of pulling his jacket on.

"Yeah." In the halogen glare I saw him clearly for the first time: medium height and build, brown wavy hair worn long, heavy eyebrows, a slightly feminine mouth. "They said—they told me—Jeremiah was dead."

"He is."

Then he nodded and began to sniffle. "I'm freezing," he said through clenched teeth. "I think I sprained my left wrist." He spat, and I saw the spittle was bloody.

"Bite your tongue when they shocked you?"

"Yeah, more than once."

"Come on. You need help?"

"I can walk. Did you really call the cops?"

"No, I was bluffing. You want me to call them?"

We were making our way back up the logging trail, slow going because I had switched off the flashlight. Jerry didn't ask why. He could figure that we made an easy target with it on. He said, "No, don't call the police. They didn't do anything."

"Kidnapping. Assault."

"How did my grandfather die?"

"It looks like a hit-and-run accident."

"You sure he's dead?"

"I just came from where it happened."

I heard him gulp back sobs in the darkness. When he spoke again, his voice was a half-octave higher, as though he had lost ten years: "You a cop?"

"I used to be a private cop. Jeremiah came to me and wanted to hire me to protect you. I didn't take him seriously. I should have."

We were getting close to where I'd left the Jeep on Route 12. Jerry said, "I don't want any of this to get in the papers."

"All right." When we reached the Jeep, no other cars were in sight. I pulled out my phone and hit the send button.

"What are you doing?"

"Trust me."

The 911 operator answered on the second ring and asked, "What is your emergency?"

"Listen," I said, putting a little of Vermont into my voice, "there's a bad drunk driver out on Route Twelve. I was just off the highway, between Montpelier and Northfield, when he came past me. I didn't see which way he turned onto Route Twelve, but he was swerving all over. Dark-colored Subaru station wagon, newer model, Vermont plate, but I couldn't make out the numbers."

"And he's on Route Twelve?"

"Has to be, he came off this road. I think you should notify the Northfield police in case he's headed south."

I gave her the other information she asked for and hung up. "Slick," Jerry said.

"It probably won't do any good, but if they get stopped we'll have a record of who the car is registered to, who's driving it. With the hit-and-run, they'll probably make an effort."

It was one side or the other of midnight. I drove Jerry back to his apartment house. He invited me in, and we walked into what might have been a monk's cell. I'd never seen a bachelor apartment as neat or as bare. I checked out Jerry's left wrist. It was swollen and bruised, but he could make a fist, touch thumb tip to each finger in turn. "I don't think anything's broken," I told him.

He got us a couple of beers and we sat on the sofa. "God, what a day," he said. He wanted to know about his grandfather. I told him what I knew.

"Well," Jerry said, finishing the last of his bottle of beer. "So. You're supposed to protect me. Thanks but no thanks. They won't catch me again."

"But they might."

He flashed me a wild-eyed look.

I asked him, "What are you afraid of?"

"You wouldn't understand. I'm not afraid of anything." He cradled his left wrist in his right hand, as though nursing a small, sick animal back to health.

"I'd think you'd like to see the people who hurt you get punished."

He stared at the floor and didn't reply.

"I could help."

He laughed without mirth and looked at me with his nose wrinkled, as though he were judging an ugly-dog contest. "How much would I owe you?"

I shook my head. "No charge. Jeremiah paid me already."

His gaze was wary, and I recognized the look of the righteous one. The monk's-cell apartment fit him: a young man unseasoned by life, still believing the world is populated by good guys and bad, white and black hats, no room for gray. I could read it in his eyes. In his estimation, if you weren't a crusader, you were for sale, you had a price, you had an ulterior motive. "You took money from my grandfather?" he asked in a harsh voice.

"A little. But he bought me with his trust."

"Yeah. Well. He's dead."

"And I owe him."

"So . . ." Jerry scratched his head. "You'd help me for free?"

"As much as I can. I'm not independently wealthy."

"But you're a PI. You charge for what you do."

"Listen to me," I said. "If I do this, I do it because Jeremiah trusted me. But if this gets big, if I face a lot of travel expenses, if I have to bring in other people, I won't have the cash to continue it."

"So I'd have to pay you."

I began to sympathize with the guy who'd hit him with the stun gun. "This isn't about payment. Mostly, it's about my wanting to know who killed your grandfather. Let's cut out the bullshit about money, OK?"

"Can I trust you?"

"I did get you out of the clearing."

"But you could be one of them, it could be a setup to make me trust you."

"Then you'd be screwed. But I'm not one of them."

"Prove it."

I grinned at him. "You want to see my Eagle Scout badge?" I got up, and he automatically reached for my empty beer bottle. He put it inside a kitchen cabinet, alongside three or four others. Abstemious little monk. "Think about it overnight," I advised him. "Are you safe here?"

"They took me about half a block from here."

"Then go stay with someone."

"You're serious?"

"Dead serious," I said. "Hop a plane. Or at least go somewhere that's not as easy to find as this place."

"I could," he said slowly. "I have some friends who wouldn't mind putting me up. But I don't want my friends hurt, and these guys know where I work, anyway, so what good's that?"

"Do you have a car?"

"Nope."

I shook my head. "Guys are chasing you, zapping you with a stun gun, they probably killed your grandfather, and they'll involve your friends if you stay with them. You're telling me you can't run away from these guys, you can't avoid them, and you can't fight them. So how are you going to stop them?"

"I could do what they want."

"What's that?"

"That's the problem," he said. "I don't know." He looked at me for a long moment, his eyes unreadable.

9

It had been a long, late evening. I crunched up the old logging road toward my cabin, fighting off a mixture of frustration and anger. Jerry's decision to stay alone in his apartment,
expressed in polite words that translated to "I don't trust you,
and you can't help me," galled me. Damn him. I had managed
to sell myself on the idea of finding the people who'd killed
Jeremiah Smith. I was fairly certain that Jerry either knew
who they were or knew the information I'd need.

I'd work on it tomorrow, I promised myself. As I topped
the last rise, I wasn't too surprised to see yellow kerosene
lamplight spilling from the windows and the faint gray billow
of smoke from the chimney. I saw a form pass by the window
and released the grip I'd instinctively taken on my gun. Sylvia
again. Just what I needed.

She opened the door as I stepped onto the shallow
porch. "Hello again," I said, stepping across the threshold.
She inclined her head and went to sit in the straight-backed
rocker, the same one she'd taken earlier. Her liquid brown
eyes flicked up to meet my gaze, and then she stared down at
the floor again.

I took a deep breath of woodstove smoke, kerosene, and some faint musk, probably perfume, though I'd never smelled anything quite like it on any other woman. It was a sensuous aroma, a rutting-animal whiff, but redolent of leaves and loam and deep shaded forest glens.

"Did you find him?" she asked in her precise way.

I plugged my cell phone into its charger, took off my jacket and tossed it on the bed, got a wine bottle and a glass and poured myself a drink. I sat down facing her. She obstinately stared at the floor as I studied her more closely than I had earlier. Her skin was odd, both young and old, flawless from a distance, but from close up scored with minute creases and wrinkles. She might have been twenty-five, she might have been fifty, on the evidence of her skin. Her face had the Asian, high-cheeked quality I'd seen in many Native Americans, but in the lamplight she seemed more European. And now I decided that her hair wasn't black after all, but an incredibly rich and deep chestnut brown.

"Thanks for feeding the stove," I said.

She nodded but did not look up.

I drank a third of my wine in one swallow. "You were right. Someone used a car to murder the old man."

She began to rock placidly, silently, casting moving shadows on the rough pine boards.

"Do you know anything else that you should tell me?" I asked.

"You will not believe me."

I handed her my glass of wine. "Try me."

She took one small sip, then returned the glass. "Some people stopped you so you would hear the old man's grandson. You went to him. You probably saved his life." She took a long breath and then let it out. Dropping her voice as if confiding a secret, she murmured, "You are a good man."

"And some bird told you that? Or a squirrel?"

She shook her head. "You cannot understand. It doesn't matter."

"Deer were standing in the road. Not people."

She folded her hands in her lap and weaved her head from side to side, but kept her eyes on the rug.

"I can't believe the deer told you, so who did? How? Cell phone? Radio?"

"It doesn't matter," she said again, and sighed.

"Maybe it's the only thing that does," I said, and that made her look at me, her brown eyes wide. "Are you talking about, about forest spirits?"

She smiled, a surprisingly childlike smile—or maybe the smile of a mother whose little one had finally said two sensible words. "You think there are spirits in the forest?"

I took another sip of wine. "Sometimes it feels that way. Especially at night."

She shook her head, now watching me closely. "No little people live out there, if that is what you are thinking. No tiny fairies or sprites or dolls or toys or cartoon characters. No what do you call them, no little elves that disguise themselves as squirrels, trees, rocks. You have to know that the animals, the plants, the rivers, mountains, the soil, are not like that, not like cartoon characters."

"OK," I said. "I won't expect a rabbit to ask me what's up."

She smiled again, as if we had shared a private joke, and then she frowned. "But everything around us does hold Spirit. Is Spirit. Even the walls, the metal in your stove, the floor. This cabin is Spirit, and all its pieces are Spirit, and it is a seamless whole. Like Squirrel. All squirrels are individual animals, and yet all are Squirrel. It is not that this bear or that bear is Grandfather. It is Bear that is Grandfather. Do you understand what I mean? Your words are difficult, like trying to shape a cup to hold water out of water itself."

"I don't know." I couldn't suppress a yawn. Black night brooded outside the windows. "I've been through times of serious thinking about spirit and souls. When my parents died, when my fiancée died, when my best friend died. My conclusion? It beats me. I may find the answer when I die myself. Or not."

"Your religion teaches you strange ideas. You believe you must die before you know Spirit?"

I gave a weary chuckle. "Religion isn't about making sense. Most believers are satisfied with 'God said it, so I believe it, and don't bother me with questions.'"

"And you meet God when you die."

I ran my finger across the window. The Thermopane—one of my upgrades when I bought it—had a small flaw, letting in moisture. It dripped from my fingertip. "Yeah, that's the idea. You meet God and he judges you."

"I think he will judge you with compassion," Sylvia said. "You offered your help. Life needs your help, here, in this place, now." In the lamplight she was startlingly attractive. I thought longingly of bed and of how many months mine had been lonely. She smiled. "I am not here to have sex with you." It was a soft, firm declaration, spoken without embarrassment or harshness.

"I didn't mean to ask you," I told her.

"No. But you did ask what you should do next with your life. I have the answer: Life needs your help, and since your life is part of all Life, it would be a good thing to offer that help. We believed you were sincere. That is why it was suggested that I talk with you, guide you if I could."

"Who suggested?"

Her expression clouded. "I'll introduce you to them when the time is right. They live nearby. All around."

"Your people?"

She sighed and rose from the chair to go. At the door she paused, hand on the knob, again avoiding eye contact. "I cannot put some things in any words you would accept or understand. But I think you can feel this: when things are out of order, or in the wrong order, the world is in disharmony."

"A few decades ago kids talked that way," I said.

"Many thousands of years ago everyone knew it without talking."

She opened the door, stepped out, and closed it behind her.

I stood, holding a half glass of wine. Sylvia exuded a primal sensuousness that aroused me, made me want to touch her, to hold her. She had a softness and a self-assurance that combined oddly in a feminine mystique so powerful that it made me feel like a kid in her presence. At times she spoke with such confidence that her words were heavy with what felt like ancient wisdom, and at other times she had the affect of a beautiful girl-child. And despite her soft refusal, a sensuous grace lived within her that made me want to be with her, to join with her in pure and primordial sex.

And yet she talked to squirrels. She didn't know how to use a phone.

I felt tipsy, but I drank another glass of wine. Then I wanted her back in the cabin with me. I threw open the door and looked out into the faint moonlight. The clouds had cracked open, and through a wide rift in them I saw overhead the glittering strip of the Milky Way, stars like diamond dust on black velvet.

"Sylvia!" The forest was silent, save only for the gentle sound of a wind through naked tree limbs, the soft rustle of pine needles. The wind was coming out of the north, pushing a cold front in. It brushed my face with a bitter touch.

I knew she had gone. Yet I stepped outside and circled the cabin, boots crunching in the snow. She wasn't hiding in the shadows. I didn't spot her tracks.

I'd spent more than half my life coming up with the right answers for people who'd paid me well. John Lincoln was fond of saying there are no real mysteries. "Somebody always knows," he had told me more than once. "Find the person who knows, and the mystery goes away."

I was quite certain that John had never met anyone like Sylvia. Completing my circuit of the cabin, I stepped up on the porch again. It was late enough, and I had drunk enough, to make me feel as if the timber under my feet were drifting on an unsteady current. "Sylvia!" I called again. "Come back. I need you."

No response. My nose ached from the cold wind.

"Screw it," I muttered. I went inside and got a pan, and took it out to a deep, clean drift, then scooped it full of snow, carried it back into the cabin, and put it on top of the stove. By tomorrow morning it would reduce to maybe a pint and a half of water.

Still cold despite the stove's warmth, I stripped to my underwear and fell into bed. I fell asleep with the sour aftertaste of wine and failure on my tongue.

10

I woke the next morning with a pounding headache from too much wine and not enough water—that and the heat in the cabin that had further dehydrated me for the first half of the night. Twice I'd risen to step outside to pee, not wanting to walk the thirty feet or so to the outhouse. Both times, as I stood shivering in the cold moonlight, having thrown on only a T-shirt, jeans, and unlaced boots, I'd felt that someone was watching me.

Easy to dismiss as wine-induced paranoia. Each time I'd stepped lively back into the warmth of the cabin and the depths of the flannel sheets and army wool blankets and had drifted back to sleep wondering if I should call Jerry. My dreams were vivid worries about his safety.

The sun woke me, lying in a bright stripe across the bed. It was still low in the sky. I guessed the time at somewhere between seven-thirty and eight, late for me. By design I'd bought no clock for the cabin, but now and again I turned on a little transistor radio to catch the news on Vermont Public Radio in low fidelity.

During my months in the cabin I'd adjusted to judging time by the fall of the light, knowing the rough times of sunrise and sunset, knowing how they changed a few minutes each day. The Earth had swung past the winter solstice just before Christmas, and now the hours of daylight were getting longer, heading toward the summer solstice in June, when the sun would come up before five in the morning and linger until nine in the evening.

Perhaps because of my elliptical conversation with Sylvia the night before, I meditated on my life and its pattern as I got the stove going, poured some of the melted snow into my Brita water filter, then heated the rest of the water and used it to wash my face and torso. Thoreau had been right: living in the forest you discover a thousand unsuspected connections to time and seasons. Winter is when you withdraw, retreat, slow down, and think and brood.

The radio told me that many people experienced this ebb into self as depression, and they even had a name for it—SAD, seasonal affective disorder. But the folks who came down with that tended to be those who spent their working days in the fluorescent rabbit-warren mazes of offices. When they retreated into themselves, they found an echoing emptiness, a vacated house.

Not so with me. John and I had always kept busy, winter and summer alike, so I'd had few opportunities to contemplate and speculate on the Meaning of It All. Still, the past months had slowed me down, accustomed me to the natural flow of time, eased me out of the tyranny of a clock that bit another small chunk out of my life each minute. I had flowed into winter, had flowed with it, had learned to greet and celebrate early darkness with a glass of wine and a good book. I had accepted winter as a season to go to sleep early and wake up late and lazy, a papa bear welcoming hibernation.

Now I'd begun to look forward to summer, expecting it would bring a contrasting energy. They'd told me stories of how the entire green state of Vermont erupts in early summer, festivals, parties, and fairs popping up as if sprung from the deep stony soil, a hectic, hilarious time as the residents release the stored-up energy of the cold months.

I finished my ablutions and combed my hair, amid the lingering scent of Dr. Bronner's Peppermint Soap. I grinned at what the old doc might have made of my philosophizing. He could have squeezed it down into a snaking passage of agate type and wrapped it around one of his bars of soap. I thought fleetingly of shaving, fingering my short beard, the product of a month away from the razor, then decided the hell with it. When in Rome.

So I poured a shot-glass of Listerine, dipped my toothbrush into it, and then dipped it into an open box of baking soda and scrubbed away the tooth-scum and hangover sourness. I rinsed with the rest of the mouthwash, then got dressed in local costume: blue flannel shirt, jeans, brown work boots.

I pulled a lemon out of the grocery bag under the table, sliced it in half, and squeezed the juice into a glass. I topped it up with water from the Brita pitcher and drank it down. My headache had mostly dissipated and my vision had cleared. I took the half-full washbasin outside and poured the dirty water into a little gully, then I scrubbed the basin clean with a couple of handfuls of snow.

Then as I turned to go back, I saw Sylvia standing motionless beneath a leafless maple right at the edge of the small clearing around the cabin. The air had become frigid, almost crystalline, the sky a deep blue dome overhead. Sylvia stood watching me, her breath condensing and drifting away over her shoulder.

I stopped, facing her, and said, "Good morning."

She simply stared for a long, silent moment, and I didn't know if she was trying to reach some big decision or was simply carefully considering her next move. She reminded me of the way the deer had deliberately stood in the roadway the evening before. At last she smiled and stepped toward me. "Good morning." She passed me and went into the cabin.

I followed, pulling the door shut behind me.

"Good to see you again." I put the bowl back into its place in the wooden washstand, realizing that I hadn't thought through what I wanted to tell her and ask her. Or maybe that wasn't so, maybe I had thought it through too much.

"Thank you."

"Where'd you go last night?"

"I have a place to sleep nearby."

"House? Trailer?"

"I have a home." She sat in the straight-backed rocker. "What did you dream about last night?"

"Don't know. Danger. Jeremiah's grandson was involved, but that's all I remember." I pulled a loaf of bread and a jar of raspberry preserves from the pantry. "Want breakfast?"

"I have eaten." She was staring at the rug again, not making eye contact. "I dreamed of times past and times to come, about my people and yours. It was sad. You really don't remember when you dream?"

I shrugged. "Sometimes I remember bits and pieces, images. My dreams are surreal and usually make no sense."

She raised an eyebrow but did not look up. "What if this is the dream? What if where you go at night when this ceases to exist for you is the reality?"

I had opened the preserves and spread a portion on a slice of seven-grain bread. "I've heard that kind of question before.

But it's pretty well established that this is what is real. Dreams are processed junk from our waking lives. How do I know this is real? It's a hell of a lot more consistent than my dreams, for one thing." I took a bite of the bread. "Sure you don't want some?"

She glanced toward my breakfast with a look of covert and lustful hunger but she said, "No, thank you."

She sat in a kind of absorbed, natural silence as I ate the bread, crunching the raspberry seeds between my molars. When I finished, I took my cast-iron snow-melting pan, went outside and filled it, and brought it back to the stove. A few drops of water hissed and sputtered as they dripped from the pan's sides onto the stovetop.

Sylvia did not look at me, but just sat and rocked. I put some gunpowder green tea in John Lincoln's old mug, the one I'd given him years earlier with the CIA logo, and carried it back to my chair, waiting for the snow to melt and the water to heat. "Anything happen last night that I should know about?"

She shrugged in an odd way, not a gesture of resignation or defiance, but more as though she was saying, *Yes, but nothing urgent,* as though it was more natural for her to shrug than to nod.

When she didn't say anything, I said, "So are you going to introduce me to your people today?"

She stiffened for a second before slipping into a more relaxed posture. "You must promise me something first." She looked me in the face, and the force of her attention struck me as something almost palpable.

"What?"

"First tell me: do you think your people are in danger? Do you think the whole human race could be—what is the thing you call it—an endangered species?"

I didn't know how to field that. For a few moments I rocked slowly, hearing the chair runners against the wood floor, the crack and pop of the logs burning in the stove. "Nuclear war could do it," I said. "Pollution, killer germs developed by the labs of three dozen nations, chemicals from genetically engineered foods. I'd say there's some element of danger. Is that what you mean?"

"There is a larger danger," she said. "A more immediate one, though it could come from any of those things. But even without any of those happening, there is a graver threat."

"What?"

"The Spirit of the world is ill. The Mother who gives us all life is weakening. If she becomes ill enough, you will all die." She leaned forward, her intense brown gaze locked on mine. "Since this time yesterday, one hundred species have become extinct forever. Millions of plants and animals have died, ending a hundred million lineages. Each came from billions of years of trial and error, birth and death, growth and change. Each species had ancestors going all the way back to the beginning of life. Each should have had descendants to carry the line to the infinite future. Every one of those hundred species that were living yesterday morning has now vanished beyond recall. No one on Earth will ever see them again. And by this time tomorrow another hundred, or maybe more, will vanish."

"I've heard that life on Earth goes through periods of great extinctions," I said. "We're seeing another one begin."

She shook her head. "Over the last seventy million years, perhaps one species went extinct every four or five years, but other species would replace them. The last time so many unique species were lost was when the great dinosaurs died. The world came close to losing all its life then."

"How do you know all this?" I asked. "You say you don't use a telephone. Have you been educated? Did you go to college?"

She looked at me in silence. Outside I heard a crow's harsh complaint and the answering chatter of a chipmunk. A log shifted in the stove and I could hear Sylvia's slow breathing, the same rhythm as her rocking chair. Dust motes floated in the slanting rays of sun coming through the east-facing window. She said slowly and with a faint tremor in her voice, "My people hear the screams and feel the pain of those who die."

I didn't know what to say.

She looked at the rug again. "Your scientists say that there have been five great extinctions on this planet since life began. We have entered the sixth." She glanced back at me. "I have not been to college. I learned this from Jeremiah Smith." She took a deep breath. "When these great deaths occur, those at the top of the pyramid of life, those who have stolen, exploited, and hoarded, will die too."

"Us?"

She nodded. "And that is why you must promise me. Will you promise to do all you can to revive and awaken the Mother?"

"I don't understand—"

"Mother Earth."

"I'm not sure what I can do." The pan on the stove made a little clatter as the water began to boil. A faint haze of steam floated above it, causing a rainbow sheen as the prismatic droplets split the sun into its component colors. "I'd be willing to promise, but one man can't—"

"That will come later," she said. "But now you must promise."

"OK, I promise to do what I can. Although I'm still not sure what that means." I frowned. "Are you—are you trying to hire me? You want me to take on a job as bodyguard to the Earth?"

I'm not sure, but I believe she smiled. "Something like that."

I had to smile too. "There are hundreds, thousands of people dedicated to saving the world, and some have millions of dollars. What can I do that they can't?"

She stood up and walked to the door, pushed it open, just a few inches, but far enough to spill in the cold air. I felt it on my cheeks and hands. She stared through the crack as if seeing something in the remote distance. "This is not about saving. Those people will fail because they are trying to save something. There is nothing to save."

"Then I don't understand."

"No." Her glance had that almost physical impact. I felt it in my chest and stomach. "You are trapped because you think the same way they do and view the world as they do. You must change first. You are, are—deaf, blind, lame. You must cure yourself first, and then you can help."

"Now I'm really confused."

She pushed the door wide open, went across the porch and down the three steps onto the snow. "Get a blanket. Put on your coat. Follow me."

WWHDTD? I suspected that Henry David would have serenely followed such a guide, perhaps to the surprise of his stodgier friend Ralph Waldo Emerson. Well, hell, I'd been patting myself on the back not so long before, seeing myself as a Thoreau for the twenty-first century. So I pulled my jacket from its peg and reached for the top blanket on the bed. Before my hand closed on it, the cell phone chimed in its charger and I picked it up to answer.

"Oakley Tyler," I said, not recognizing the number.

"Jerry Smith," he said. His voice sounded unsteady. "I'm at the office, at my paper. Look, I need to talk with you about your investigating my grandfather's death."

"When?"

I heard him sigh. "I can meet you in Montpelier. The diner at the corner of State and Main. I need some time to clear my desk. Noon?"

"If I'm not there at the stroke, wait for me."

"No problem. You'll find me there."

I grabbed the green wool army blanket and draped it over my shoulder. Then something made me leave the phone connected to its charger, though the battery should have already been full. Somehow I did not think that Sylvia, or Henry David, would approve of it. I stepped out into the freezing morning air.

11

Sylvia was walking away from me, into the forest. The sky arched a deep clear blue overhead. Above the treetops I made out the distant shape of Burnt Mountain, twenty miles east of us, looking as if it were no more than a mile away: the air was so cold that the moisture had frozen out of it, leaving it as deceptively transparent as the air of the high desert.

I floundered a little when we hit a series of drifts, but ahead of me Sylvia didn't even seem to notice the change in snow depth. She walked on, surefooted, not even sinking into the snow, not even crunching the crust as I did. Her walk had that lithe fluidity of a Native American, taking all the weight on the whole foot, not coming down heel-first and punching through as I did. And I doubted that she weighed more than a hundred pounds, a lot less than my one-eighty.

Though the air felt well below zero, the sun was warm on my face. She led me through hardwood growth and around a stand of pines until we came to the same outcrop of rocks where I'd first met her. She stopped and said, "Spread out the blanket. We'll sit on it."

I did as she asked and she sat, facing the river, somewhere down there below us. I knocked snow from my boots and sat beside her, cross-legged. I could smell the deer hide she wore, the odor bringing me images of a night forest, animals panting from having run a long way, a fawn nuzzling her mother's teats, eager for the warm milk.

Sylvia sat quiet and immobile, her breath slow, spine straight, gazing ahead at the treetops down the slope, where the forest floor slanted down to the river. I wanted to talk, but I didn't think she'd welcome that. I began to shiver. Here the trees shaded us, and I missed the warm touch of the sun.

After what might have been two or three minutes, though it seemed longer, she said softly, "Do you see what is around you?"

I kept my voice as low as hers: "I see the forest. I see some places where the snow has drifted or melted and the ground shows through. I see where the snowmelt froze over there, making a little rivulet of ice. I can't see the river, though I think I can hear it under the ice."

"So would you say we are surrounded by nature?"

"I might."

"And you know that in the distance are roads, houses, and cities, stores and businesses." She paused. "Telephone poles and electric wires. Airplanes. Cars."

"Yes."

"Imagine that none of those things actually exist. There is only this nature, this wilderness, and it covers the entire world, each climate and place different. Forests give way to savannas, jungles huddle against mountains, volcanoes steam and rumble, the seas wash the shores of islands, but nowhere is there anything built by humans."

"OK." It wasn't easy, but I tried.

After a moment she said, "Now it is a later time. Now there are people out there, small clans who move from place to place and live in tepees or mud homes or even in caves. It would take a week to walk between one settlement and another. We are here but we are, in any meaningful sense, alone."

"Adam and Eve," I said.

She rocked her right hand side to side in her "no" gesture. "We are not the first people. There have always been people of one sort or another, and there always will be people. But none of them are here now. Here there are only you and me, and perhaps a few of our relatives are a day's walk away. And all around is this that you call nature. Now can you imagine that?"

I gazed downhill, and in my imagination the road that had been bulldozed through the forest and around the hills filled in with vegetation, went back to woods. My car vanished. Route 12 vaporized and the trees reclaimed it. The houses turned to mist and drifted away. I envisioned the whole state of Vermont reverting to wilderness, and saw the wilderness spread across all of New England and Eastern Canada, and before it went a green wave that swallowed nearly all the humans and every trace of modern life. "I can imagine that."

"See the entire world in its primal state." Her voice sounded joyful, like someone remembering a happy time.

And so I did, letting the wild spread over the continent, then over the planet: cities, roads, airports all vanishing, millions of people evaporating. The world was as it had been twenty thousand years ago. And then a terrible solitude gripped me and I said, "We're alone."

"Yes."

I had an absurd moment of existential panic, as though I had somehow, by an act of will and imagination, erased all of modern civilization. I glanced up at the pieces of sky I could see between bare interlacing limbs, hoping to see a jet or at least a vapor trail, but I looked into a blue abyss.

"You are feeling how it would be if you had really made the world of men vanish," she said simply.

"It feels very lonely," I replied. I felt a curious division: part of me was five years old and worried about stepping on a crack and breaking my mother's back, and the other was a detective, an adult who looked at my childish fears and smirked, hiding his own concerns.

"Now how will we survive?" Sylvia asked suddenly. "We need food, shelter, warmth, medicine, tools."

"We could hunt."

"With no guns or technology. You are born naked. Your parents must make your clothing from the stuff the world around us provides, the world you call nature."

"We could make spears. Bows and arrows."

"What would you hunt? Where are the animals you would hunt?"

She made me acutely aware that for some time I had heard no bird sounds, no crows. No chatter of chipmunks. "I don't know. We'd have to go find them."

"What if there are not enough animals for us to find? Not enough to keep us alive for the winter?"

"Dig for roots," I suggested. "Find what kinds of bark we can eat, things like that."

"And if there is not enough of that?"

"Then we'd starve." I tried to say it lightly, brushing off a hypothetical problem, but in my stomach I felt a knot of certainty: without game or any other source of food, I might live a few weeks, but I didn't have a lot of stored fat. In a matter of a month or less I would die. Nothing moved anywhere around us. I couldn't see anything that looked remotely edible.

Sylvia whispered, "Yes, we would starve." She gave me that intense brown gaze of hers again. "If we have no hope, we could walk for three days to my family's camp. They will share their food with us. They will never withhold food, though they have enough only for themselves. We would then all starve, though we might prolong our own lives for a few weeks."

"If it came to that," I said, "I would say we shouldn't find your people and take what little they have just to gain a few more days of life."

"Why?"

I struggled to find the words, but settled for "It wouldn't be a kind thing to do."

"No," she agreed. She let the silence stretch out. I wondered why she was putting me through this exercise, but it had become clear that if she had anything to teach me, she would instruct me only on her own terms. I sank into her silence, but I kept looking around, wondering how long it would be before a squirrel or wild turkey or deer would wander into sight. If I saw such a creature, then the speculation meant nothing. There would be a source of food, a source of life.

But what if there really was nothing to eat? When I was a teenager, I had read the Lewis and Clark diaries. According to them, once deer roamed the forests and fields in herds that numbered into the thousands. Now spotting one beside the road was enough to thrill a van full of tourists. I had heard that nine out of every ten Vermont hunters came home empty-handed every November.

"If this forest," Sylvia suddenly broke in, "were our supermarket, our only food supply, what would be the most important thing we could do with it?"

"Conserve it."

"What do you mean?"

The chill had seeped into my legs, and I was shivering. I wondered how she could seem so comfortable, dressed as lightly as she was. "We'd . . . take only what we needed, and we'd leave behind everything else. To reproduce, to increase, so it would be there later for us, for our children."

"Yes. That is the imperative of noninterference. That is the first law of . . . conscious nature. The part of nature that exercises free will. Animals."

"The imperative of noninterference," I repeated. "When the white man came, he found plains filled with buffalo, forests rich with herds of deer, enormous flocks of wild turkeys, streams so full of fish that the water itself seemed alive. The settlers thought the Native Americans were stupid, letting all those resources go to waste. But it wasn't wasted was it? That was the stock ready to go on the shelves of your supermarket."

"Not just theirs," she said. "It supplied food for all living things, not just humans. If you had enough and made sure there was always some excess, then when hard times came you would be ready. And you must not interfere. That is most important. When humans interfere with the cycles of nature, with the life of the world, you distort the way things are, pervert the intent of the Creator."

"And what about farming?" I asked. "Clear some forest, grow corn, beans, whatever."

"Some of the early people did this," Sylvia acknowledged. "Others thought it was a violation of the law of noninterference. When people became totally dependent on the things they grew, they created a terrible imbalance. Their food increased, and they multiplied. They took the forests and changed them into more human beings, but hunger begets hunger, and they began to eat the world around them. They needed always more land and more, and so they fought other humans to take their land, to remove their competition for food. Many among those who grew and stored food died in battle."

"But those who hunted and gathered didn't fight wars?"

"Not often, except when the farmers attacked them, or when there were huge, terrible changes in weather that forced them to move hundreds of miles to search for food. But as a rule they lived and died in the hands of the gods, surrendering themselves to the ways of the Earth, even during times of drought or famine. It is more correct, more . . . more noble, you might say, to surrender to necessity and die than to interfere."

"That's a tough law, that noninterference law."

She did not seem to hear me. "It holds even with your own family, maybe especially with them. Never interfere. That is the reason many Native Americans even today will not offer advice or tell you how you should live. If you ask them to advise you, you make them uncomfortable. Many avoid advising you by telling you stories instead."

"Even Jesus used parables to teach wisdom." A childhood Methodist memory floated into my mind, and I quoted, " 'And He taught them in parables.' He told them . . . not to 'gather up food in barns.' "

"Yes," Sylvia said, and then we lapsed back into silence. It was easy to imagine that her fantasy was true, that we were the only humans for miles around in a world still in its natural state. But what was interference, really? Where was the boundary? I asked, "Is it interference to build a tepee or to drag dried grass into a cave to sleep on? Is it interference to fell trees and build a cabin?"

She tilted her right hand back and forth. "Birds build nests, bears have their dens. To have a home is not interference, but the way of nature, with humans as with the other people."

"Yet we should walk lightly upon the Earth."

She looked pleased. "That is a good thing to say."

"And many are trying to do it. They tell us we must preserve the wilderness so future generations will have it."

"No, that is arrogance," she said. "It is not good if people believe the world is here only for them. It is not good to save it only so their children can use it." She gave me a challenging look. "Tell me, do you believe that all creation has been made only for humans?"

The sun had climbed higher, and though I was still numb, shafts of sunlight were at least providing an illusion of warmth. I thought for a minute and then said, "I guess I don't see much difference. Either the world is here for us to use, or else we've claimed it all for our use. It's the same either way."

She grunted, frowned in thought, and then said, "You know there are people who believe that everyone else is out to harm them?"

"Paranoids."

"Paranoids. It is a kind of . . . illness of the mind."

"Yes. They have delusions."

"Have you ever known such a person?"

"Yes." I wiggled my left toes, feeling through the cold the pull of the scar tissue. "There was a Turkish man in Germany who had built up a kind of criminal empire. His name was Ahmed, and though there were plenty of people who wouldn't have minded him dying, he really did think that everyone was trying to kill him. He kidnapped a woman from

America, and her company hired John Lincoln and me to get her back."

"And did you?"

I tasted the sour tang of bile, remembering the glissando of Ahmed's screams when he plunged out of the hotel window and impaled himself on a spear held by a monumental bronze statue in the courtyard below. "I got her back."

She stared at me, and when I did not meet her gaze, she said, "You killed him."

"Indirectly."

"And you did it to save someone else."

"That's part of what I do. Or what I used to do."

She rocked back and forth, making a soft cooing noise in her throat, like a mother comforting a child. "And how was this man's world, this Ahmed's world, constructed? Was he at the center of it?"

"Yes, he was," I said, glimpsing her intention. "Ahmed simply assumed that everything everyone did was because of him. I'd say he thought of himself as not just the center of his world, but of the real world, the whole world."

"And that is a mental illness. But how is it different from thinking that everything in the world is made just for you?"

"At least looking on the world as something made for people is positive, not negative."

"It is the same perception. Remember what I said about how the individual squirrels are still Squirrel? The individual humans are Human. And if Human thinks the world is made for Human, then everyone is sharing the illness."

My bones were aching from cold. "That's one way of looking at it. But what does this have to do with Jeremiah Smith?"

"The knowledge I offer you is at the center of it all." She glanced downhill, in the direction of the river. "People are suffering a delusion, a mental illness. The whole world is for them, the whole universe is created only for them. They are insane, and they will kill those who do not agree to their insanity, those who have wakened from the delusion and the dream."

She seemed to want me to say something. I said, "I read once a story about the Buddha. Someone asked him if he were a god, and he said no. 'Then are you an angel?' He still said no. 'Then what are you?' And he said, 'I am awake.'"

"He was a wise man."

"I guess he was. Are you telling me that Jeremiah was killed because he was—was spiritually enlightened?"

"Was he martyred, you mean? No. But he was, as you say, awake. Some people dream they are awake, but they still are dreaming. Others really do awaken."

"Lucid dreaming," I said. "I've had that a few times, mostly when I was a kid. You're half awake, but still asleep enough to dream and to direct yourself in the dream. I used to fly."

She smiled and laid a hand on my knee, not affectionately, but just as though she felt we had to make contact. "Yes," she said softly. "In my dreams I become a bird when I'm awake-while-dreaming."

"No, not a bird," I said as she removed her hand with a sudden self-consciousness. "I'm still human. I used to fly like Superman."

"It is better as a bird," she said. "You would like it. Other than the predator birds like owls, most see from the sides of their heads, like deer, and their vision is sharp. They see more of the world than you do." She sighed. "Prey animals see almost the whole world. Predators only look straight ahead. Humans look straight ahead. Try being a bird. It lets you see the world differently."

"If I ever have another lucid dream, I'll try."

Sylvia picked up a twig and ran her fingers along it. Her nails were short and smooth, her hands young and strong. "When the First People came to live here, they fought, but then they rediscovered the Great Laws. They lived in balance for ten thousand years." She dropped the twig. "Then came the Europeans, people who were lost in their dream. They dreamed they were gods, that the world was theirs. They could do anything they wanted to the world and to the First People, because they believed there would be no consequences. But that was part of the dream."

"More like a nightmare, the way you tell it."

"They raped Mother Earth, murdered the First People, enslaved their own people. Now the richest and most powerful live as gods. Even the slaves in your culture believe that if they fall into the same dream they will become as gods themselves, or their children will. But that is part of the nightmare. Most of the First People who survive have adopted that dream, too. And when they fail to become like the Europeans, they escape into other dreams, fueled by alcohol, drugs, and violence. But a few have not fallen asleep. The world around them has changed, and though they are still awake, they at least know they are living in the dream world."

"You're telling me that I'm asleep too."

"Only if you believe the nightmare. But you know you are not a god. The others think they are the center of the world and they can interfere all they want without consequences. You do not share that madness. Nor did Jeremiah Smith." She closed her eyes. "His wife was awake. She knew. She wakened him."

"She was an Abenaki."

"Yes, one of the ones who stayed awake while the land fell into the European dream. Jeremiah used to walk in the forest. He talked with my people."

"With you?"

"I was there. I have heard his voice. He was a good man."

I hesitated to ask the question, maybe afraid that it would wake me or put me to sleep, but I did: "Can you tell me who killed him?"

"Dreamers," she said. "Ones who know in a way they are dreaming and who will kill to keep from awakening."

"Give me a name."

"I cannot." She turned the top half of her body toward me. "If I did, that would be interference."

"And if I find the murderers myself?"

"Predators look forward," she said simply. "It is not interference. It is what they do."

Before I could protest that she hadn't answered me, she raised her right hand in a sudden gesture of warning. Her nose wrinkled as if she had caught an unpleasant odor.

"What?" For some reason I whispered.

She leaned forward again, turning her head side to side. The motion pulled her deerskin shirt tight, showing me she wore nothing under it. The cold had made her nipples erect, and her left breast showed in a contour under the deerskin. And then food, prey, came at last into my vision, and I felt ludicrously relieved that we would not starve after all: a pair of deer came crashing uphill from the river, bounding through the brush below us, on the fringe of the heaviest forest. They crossed and vanished into the shelter of the woods, a six-point buck and a doe that looked as if she might be heavy with young. They were running from something.

"He is coming," Sylvia said.

12

W ho is it?" I asked.

Sylvia tilted her head in the direction from which the deer had come, so still that I thought she was holding her breath. I looked down, through brush and scattered trees. I caught a glint of light on metal and then two figures resolved out of the background, two men wearing camouflage. Both carried rifles. They might have been halfway between us and the river. I took the Police Special from my jacket pocket and held it between my legs, folding a corner of the blanket over to conceal it.

The two halted fifty feet away, as though they had just noticed me sitting there so still. They both wore caps that shadowed their faces, but the larger one was Bill Grinder and the other was slighter and, from the way he moved, younger.

They paused only for a moment, and then as they toiled up the last, steepest part of the climb, I saw that the other man was probably between twenty-five and thirty, skinny and sallow. Wispy blond hair escaped from his hunting cap at the temples, and as they got even closer I could see the craters of ancient acne across his cheeks.

"You're on my land," I said loudly when they were close enough.

The kid looked startled, as though he'd been caught doing something he shouldn't.

"Hell, Tyler, we're huntin'," Grinder said. His tone was defiant, confrontational. He had taken the point, and behind him and to his right the kid shifted his rifle. I thought he had just thumbed off the safety.

"Deer season ended in November."

"Rabbit season runs to April," Grinder said.

As if that inspired him, the kid said, "We're hunting rabbits," reminding me irresistibly of Elmer Fudd.

"Maybe so, but this is private property," I told them.

Grinder laughed, a liquid, phlegmy sound, and the kid gave me a weak, oddly apologetic grin. Grinder spat and said, "Maybe it's different down in cracker land where you come from, but here you gotta have permission to stop me. You don't want hunters, you have to file a request with the town and pay a license fee, and you gotta post the land with signs in your name."

"I've lived here long enough to know that rabbits aren't plentiful here. So why'd you pick my place to hunt?"

Grinder didn't meet my eyes. "Saw tracks here when I came for Jeremiah's truck. Lot of 'em. Rabbits all over the place."

"I don't care if they're having the North American rabbit convention here. I don't want hunters on my land, Bill."

"Yeah, but you can't stop us. Law's on our side."

"Bill, I'm telling you to get off my land."

"You can't order us off. We're hunters, and hunters can go wherever they want in Vermont and shoot anything in season. Only exceptions are inside town limits or where the land's been registered and posted. Your place ain't either."

"I put up No Hunting signs during deer season. They were all torn down inside a week."

"'Cause you ain't registered with the town. I checked. So the signs wouldn't have counted anyway. You don't like it, take it up with the NRA."

The younger man was shifting from foot to foot, looking increasingly edgy. I asked, "Who's the kid, Bill?"

"Darryl helps me in the shop sometimes," Grinder said. "Darryl, this here's Oakley Tyler. They wrote stories about him in the magazines and all."

Darryl relaxed and muttered, "Pleased t'meetcha."

I nodded at him. "You didn't happen to be in the woods out here the other day, did you, Darryl? With that rifle?"

"No, sir!" He took a step back and his rifle barrel, pointed vaguely at the ground three feet in front of his feet, rose toward me fractionally. "No, sir," he said again. "That wasn't me."

"What's your full name?" I asked.

Bill stepped sideways, cutting off my view of Darryl. "That's enough, boy," he said without looking around. "OK, Mr. Tyler, you don't want us to hunt, we won't hunt—this time. We'll head out the same way we came in. But if we see a rabbit, well, you might hear a gun go off." He kept the tone easy, but it held an edge of threat.

The two of them went down the slope, moving faster with the pull of gravity helping instead of resisting them. Beside me Sylvia exhaled noisily, and I realized she'd said not a word, that she'd been absolutely still, the whole time.

"Funny they didn't speak to you," I said.

She ran her right hand across the top of her leg, over the deerskin. I could see now that she was shivering. "If you keep very still, you become invisible."

I laughed, but she didn't smile at all. "You're serious?"

"Sometimes it doesn't work," she granted, taking a deep breath.

I shook my head. "They seemed surprised to see me," I said. "I think they just didn't get around to noticing you. I wonder what they're looking for."

She flared her nostrils and sniffed the air. "That is not for me to know. It is your matter."

I took the Police Special from beneath the fold of the blanket. She looked away as if it were obscene, and I dropped it back into my jacket pocket. I asked, "Did they frighten you?"

She gave me a flat look that said, *Of course they did.*

"I'm sorry."

"I am not used to being so close to hunters." She pronounced "hunters" the way a devout peasant in the Middle Ages might have mouthed the name of a demon—fearfully.

"They're gone now," I said. "Or well on their way. All right. Are you going to take me to meet your people?"

"Not now. They do not like hunters. They have gone."

"I don't think those were really hunters." I got up and stretched my legs, numbed by the position I had been sitting in and by the cold. I walked down to the spot where Grinder and Darryl had paused and studied the tracks. Generic hunting or winter boots. Only Grinder's were large enough to belong to the shooter, but he couldn't have been. He wouldn't have had time to return to his garage and get to my place so soon after taking Jeremiah's call.

I turned to ask Sylvia what she knew about those two guys.

She was gone. She had faded into the wilderness as if she had never been there at all.

13

I found the offices of *This Week* on the second floor of a brick building on Main Street in Montpelier. I arrived at eleven-thirty by the newsroom clock and stood in the doorway, watching three people busy in the huge open room that must once have been warehouse space for the stores below.

Five chipped and splintered wooden desks stood haphazardly around the room, like cows that had strayed into a pasture too large for comfort. Against the arched front windows a light table and drawing table stood side by side, and the whole far wall was lined by filing cabinets and stacked cardboard file boxes. I guessed that the reception area was where I stood, marked by a frayed orange sofa leaking stuffing from the corners and three uncomfortable-looking chairs.

Across from me a young man with a sandy ponytail sat at the drawing table, aligning computer-generated text and ads on tabloid-sized sheets of bluelined, wax-coated layout paper. It struck me that this production method was for all practical purposes as outdated as the Linotype machine.

Past the young man, at the farthest desk, a shorthaired woman in the nebulous territory around thirty-five leaned forward, staring intently at a computer screen and typing with a machine-gun rhythm. She wore jeans and a vivid red sweat-shirt, and from her expression she hated whatever news she was typing.

The last staffer was an Asian woman midway between the others, talking on the phone. She held up a finger to tell me she'd be with me soon. The other two noticed her, gave me a quick glance, and returned to work. I didn't see Jerry Smith.

"No," the woman on the phone said loudly. "No, we only mentioned two of your brands. We didn't dis the company itself. No—that's nuts! We can print anything we want about a politician, but if we mention a corporation, you try to come down on us like a piano off a third-floor balcony! No retraction."

She listened impatiently and said, "Don't tell me about the Supreme Court. Maybe they have ruled that corporations have the same rights as citizens, but no, this is way past that. We'll treat them as public figures, but they have to live by the same rules as the politicians they buy and sell every day." She rolled her eyes in exasperation. "You do that. Let us know."

She hung up the phone so emphatically that I thought she might have broken it.

She came toward me pushing her black hair away from her eyes. "Can you believe that? Threatening to sue us because we mentioned their products! Same company that contributed money to that damn PAC that ran ads in a dozen papers claim-ing the president had a secret gay relationship with the Speaker of the House."

"Audacious of them," I said.

"Hell of a lot worse than that. Death of the First Amend-ment, that's what it is. Free speech in this country is dying. The corporations have their hands on its throat and they won't let go."

"Tough time to be a journalist," I agreed. "I came to see Jerry Smith."

"I haven't seen him this morning, but I didn't get in until ten. He mostly works from home, though."

"The editor or the publisher in?"

She threw a thumb over her shoulder at the woman on the computer. "Gina Berkof. Editor and publisher."

I went over to Gina's desk and, detecting me with peripheral vision or internal radar, she muttered, "Just a sec, just a sec."

She bent back from the keyboard like Ray Charles hitting a good melodic run, rattled the keys for another minute, then struck the Enter key with a flourish.

"Done." She smiled at me, a medium-large woman, her light brown hair cropped in a unisex cut, her face the cherubic kind that brought to mind good times and old friends. I gave her an appreciative look that I think she noticed. By fashion-model standards she was at least thirty pounds overweight, but her body had a lushness that probably had become that way after a childhood of baby-fat loveliness. Warm brown eyes, straight nose, slightly dimpled chin, and full, smiling lips. Rubens would have taken one look at her and reached for his palette.

She tilted her head. "Now tell me you're a corporate lawyer," she challenged.

"Not guilty. You the boss?"

"Editor, publisher, and I also sweep out the place on Fridays." She looked straight at me with those strong, soft eyes. "Sit down and tell me what I can do for you—as long as you're not selling anything."

She sat at her desk, I took a chair pulled up beside it. "I'm looking into the death of Jerry Smith's grandfather."

"Police?" she asked without inflection. I would hate to play poker against her.

"No. Just doing a favor for a friend."

"Friend have a name?"

"Jeremiah Smith."

"He's dead."

"That's why I'm making sure to do him the favor."

"All right," she said. She tilted her head. "You know Jerry too, then?"

"I met him last night for the first time. Do you know where I could find him?"

"He has a desk here, but mostly he e-mails his work in. Sometimes he goes to New York and visits friends. If you mean at the moment, let me check. Guys! Seen Jerry today?"

The pony-tailed young man said, "He was here early. Left a few minutes before you came in, Gina, didn't say where he was heading."

She turned back to me. "I'll give him a message for you if you want," she said, picking up a blue pencil with a yellow brass cap instead of an eraser and pulling a yellow legal pad across the desk. "What's your name?"

"Tyler, Oakley Tyler." I spelled it for her.

"What's your business?"

"Retired."

"No, really?" She grinned. "They replaced you yet? I want that job."

So I explained about John Lincoln's death and about how I was taking time off. "I'm not licensed in this state," I said, "but as I told you, this is just a favor for a friend."

"You and Jeremiah Smith were friends?"

I smiled. She probably knew something about the kind of friends Jeremiah would or would not have. "Acquaintance. Can you tell me anything I might not know about his death?"

"Just a sec." She pulled the phone over, used the brass tip of the pencil to punch in a number. Into the receiver, she said, "Jerry. Guy named Oakley Tyler is here. He says he knew your grandfather. Call when you get this message." She hung up. "He's not at home."

I looked at the clock. "I'm meeting him in ten minutes for lunch."

"Then why come here?"

"I just wanted to see where he worked, wanted to ask if the paper had any inside stuff on Jeremiah that hadn't been published."

"I'm sorry, but I only know what I read in the daily paper this morning."

"I read it too," I said. "Three paragraphs, ending with the police quoted as saying they had no clues."

"We don't normally investigate crime news. Weekly, you know."

"The day before Jeremiah was hit he told me he thought Jerry's life was in danger, too. Any insights about that?"

Gina leaned back in her chair and exhaled a substantial breath. "I don't know anything about his personal life. He covers politics and does music reviews for us, mostly, and he's never panned a politician or a performer badly enough to draw a threat against his life." Her smile was strained. "I always thought Jerry was overeducated for this job. He has a good degree in science, but he says he burned out on that in college. He makes his living writing for us and freelancing for magazines all over the country."

"What's he been covering lately?"

She tapped the pencil on the desk. "Nothing dangerous, nothing out of his usual line. You talked to the police about all this?"

"They weren't eager to accept my help."

"They wouldn't consider it part of their job description to satisfy curiosity seekers or ex-PIs."

"True," I said. "Well, I'd better see if Jerry's waiting for me at the diner down the street." But as I pushed up from the creaking chair, I asked, "Can you tell me anything about any Native Americans who live out in the woods near Northfield?"

She raised her arched eyebrows. "What? No."

I had one more question. "Do you know Caleb Benson?"

Gina froze. "Not personally," she said through stiff lips.

"I met him, very briefly. What can you tell me about him?"

She sniffed. "Richest man in town. Maybe in the state. Owns twenty to thirty thousand acres of timberland up in the Northeast Kingdom, all along the Canadian border and into New Hampshire. Inherited land from his parents and became a lumber baron."

"How did his parents come to own that much land?"

She took a moment to square three pieces of paper on her desk. "It's a matter of public record. His father bought it piecemeal."

"Did Benson know Jeremiah?"

She guffawed. "Not socially, certainly. Opposite ends of the spectrum—economic, political, and so on. Benson's in his fifties, and Jeremiah was twenty years older. Did Benson know of Jeremiah? Probably. He was a character, a crotchety old coot, and I say that with all due respect." She lowered her voice. "And if you suspect Benson had something to do with Smith's death, keep that to yourself. Stay out of Benson's way. It's never a good idea to harass a rich man, and Benson's known to have a short fuse."

"Do you have any stories on Benson in your morgue?"

"Sure, but it's mostly glad-hand stuff, with grip and grin photos. A year or two ago we did run something about how he didn't string along with the big timber companies. They were threatening to post their land against hunters if the state government didn't offer them tax breaks. That might be the only semicritical piece we ever ran on him, at least the only one where we had a sort of editorial sneer, if you know what I mean."

"Did Jerry write that piece?"

"No, I did."

So much for my tingling Spidey sense. "OK, before I leave, could you give me a quick profile of Benson?"

She looked up toward the ceiling and rattled off her answer as if she were rat-tatting it into a computer: "Smart guy, graduated from Harvard, a biochemistry major. His daddy meant for him to be a politician, but that went out the window when the old man died. Reclusive. Some people call him a crank, but since he's rich they express that as 'eccentric.'" She leaned back, tapping her pencil against her chair arm. "Nasty temper. I saw him close up only one time, and he was screaming then. Political rally in front of the statehouse protesting clear-cutting. Benson is not exactly an environmentalist." She rose. "I wrote that piece, too, although it was pretty straight reporting. I'll have Sandra dig them up and copy the articles if you want."

"I'd also like copies of any political stories Jerry Smith has done."

"We'll give you a sampler."

"Thanks." Her handshake was quick and firm. "I appreciate your giving me the time."

"No problem. Be careful, and if you quote me, I'll deny everything."

"I won't." I told her I'd be back in an hour for the copies of the stories and at nearly twelve-thirty, I left. If he hadn't become tired of waiting, if they hadn't snatched him again, Jerry should be looking for me at the diner on the corner.

14

A t one time I was the kind of guy who made a point of punctuality, as if expecting a gold star. I found the Coffee Corner Diner two minutes after leaving the newspaper office and walked in expecting to find an impatient Jerry at a table, but he wasn't there yet. I asked a waitress if there was a vacant booth.

"One in the back," she said, and guided me to a booth where I could see the entire length of the place, with a row of red vinyl-covered booths on the left, a long counter with chrome and plastic stools on my right. It was fairly busy.

I scored a cup of coffee and two sections from the *Boston Globe*, and sat sipping and reading for at least fifteen minutes. Then, to my surprise, Sandra from the paper walked in, saw me, and came back to the booth.

She tossed a fairly thick envelope on the table. "Enjoy. I've got to get some take-out."

She went to the counter, where the counterman apparently knew what she wanted already. He handed her a hefty white paper bag and a cardboard tray with three cups. She balanced them and left the diner as I opened the envelope.

Inside were photocopies of twelve stories. Jerry's byline was on all but one of them. The first was an article lambasting the idea of genetically modified crops. Sandra had thrown in two movie reviews and several editorial pieces critical of corporate lobbying activities in the State House, unsigned but with "JS" written in pale blue and circled in the corners. There was an offprint of an article from the *New Englander* magazine, a well-written piece about the environmental movement, pointing out strengths and weaknesses in a very even-handed manner.

The story of Caleb Benson's blow-up, written by Gina, downplayed the event, making it sound more like a polite exchange of ideas than a shouting match. Her piece on his publicly opposing the timber companies, on the other hand, suggested that he knew they were going to back down anyway and was just doing it to burnish his image.

At about one, I looked up and saw Jerry pushing his way through the now-crowded diner, his expression grim. I had already reached the conclusion that whatever was going on probably had no relation to anything he'd written. But it might have something to do with a piece he had yet to publish.

He slid into the booth opposite me. Today he wore L. L. Bean Velcro-tabbed blue tennis shoes, heavy and waterproof enough for walking in snow, a soft pea-green cotton shirt, and a new-looking down-filled navy blue ski jacket. He stood up to peel off the jacket and toss it onto the seat before settling down again opposite me.

"Sorry I'm late." He looked away from me and muttered, "I had to make the funeral arrangements."

"Will there be a service?"

Jerry shook his head. "Grandpa once told me he didn't want a funeral. So many of his friends had died that he came to despise memorial services." He shrugged. "But four or five people have let me know they'd like to speak a few words, remember him, that kind of thing. I guess it doesn't matter to Grandpa now. It's for his friends, not him. So I'm planning to have something, but just not a regular funeral."

"Maybe a memorial service in a local church."

Jerry barked once in surprised laughter. "The only one Grandpa would set foot in, and probably the only one that didn't mind him coming, was the Unitarian. I left a message on their machine this morning. They may help me put something together."

"What about the body?"

"The police said it would be released to me today. I think I'll have him cremated and sprinkle the ashes over the woods from a light plane." He noticed a flicker in my expression. "What's wrong?"

I shook my head, not wanting to mention my promise to return John Lincoln's ashes to the green land he treasured in memory. "Nothing. Is there a will?"

"I haven't found one."

"I'll help if I can," I said. "I just arranged a funeral myself last summer."

"Thanks, man." He took a deep breath. "OK. So we're meeting. So what do you want to know?"

"You really didn't recognize the two men in the woods?"

"No. And I don't want you to pursue it, either. What happened is my business, not yours."

"I've made a living out of being discreet."

He set his jaw in a stubborn way. "But if you poked around, word would get out, believe me. I don't want anyone to know what happened."

"Got it. Do you know a blond kid, midtwenties, named Darryl?"

"Nope."

"Do you know Bill Grinder, a mechanic? He was acquainted with your grandfather."

"Grinder's lived around these parts forever," Jerry said. "I've spoken to him maybe twice, and the last time—" He broke off, frowning.

"Spit it out," I said. "I'm on your side."

He shook his head. "It was a few months ago. Grandpa picked me up in his old truck because he said he wanted some company. He does—did that sometimes. He drove over to Caleb Benson's house first. I had no idea they even knew each other. Maybe they didn't. We didn't see Benson, but a blonde woman about my age answered the door and told Grandpa that Benson wasn't seeing anybody and he should call for an appointment. Grandpa called her Benson's bimbo, but I think it might have been his third wife. Grandpa said he married someone a lot younger. They keep mostly to themselves. For that matter, it's odd that he's been in town over the winter. He usually leaves for Sarasota in October and doesn't come back until April."

"Your grandfather asked me if Benson had me on his payroll."

"Did he tell you what happened after our visit to Benson's house?"

"No. What happened?"

His eyes moved as if he were reading the story. "It gets weirder. From Benson's place we drove to Grinder's garage. We get out and Grandpa goes in and starts talking to Grinder, who's on a creeper underneath an old Buick. Grandpa sort of talked to his legs, asked him if he'd ever heard of gene-jumping. He say anything to you about that?"

"Maybe it's better if you can honestly say you have no idea what your grandfather told me. What is gene-jumping?"

Jerry shrugged. "Grandpa was big into biology and forestry. He did some work for the state as a forester. And Grandma was passionate about trees. She used to tell me they had their own intelligence."

"Spirit," I corrected.

"Yeah, that was her word," Jerry said softly.

"So what did Grinder say when your grandpa asked him that question?"

"Acted like he didn't know what Grandpa was talking about. Said the only 'jeans' he'd ever heard of jumping were the ones fat women wore, something like that. Grandpa cussed a little and we left. I thought Grandpa was getting a little— overworked, you know. Happens sometimes when people get old, they develop delusions."

"Were Grinder and Jeremiah friends?"

"This is a small community, the whole reach from Montpelier to all those little towns south of us. People who've lived here a while pretty much get to know everybody else. I don't know if Grinder was one of Grandpa's buddies. I can't tell you when they met, anything like that, but they seemed to know each other all right. I guess when Grandpa worked for the town Grinder was the guy who repaired the trucks. Grandpa talked like they'd known each other for a long time, but not like they were particularly friendly."

"So that term, gene-jumping," I said. "Can you explain it?" A waitress was approaching.

"It doesn't mean anything."

"Humor me. Lunch is on me."

Jerry shrugged. "I'll try. But if you want, you can ask at the paper and they'll give you an article I wrote about it last year. I think that might be what put the notion into Grandpa's head to begin with."

I nodded, not mentioning that I had the article in the brown envelope sitting on the seat beside me.

We ordered sandwiches—he asked for his usual—and as the waitress walked away, I said, "Give me the quick version."

He cracked his knuckles. "You know what genes are?"

"They carry DNA," I said. "They're why my eyes are brown, that kind of thing?"

"Yeah, in a quick-and-dirty way, that's right. Actually, though, they don't carry DNA, they're made of it. And DNA is just long chains of amino acids on a rail of sugar. They carry the code of life in clusters called chromosomes. They have a kind of blueprint for everything that makes you you. Not just people, but every other living thing."

"So how do they jump?"

His expression intensified. "That's where it gets . . . interesting. You know how *E. coli* has become a problem in the states?"

"Bacteria, isn't it? Causes hamburger recalls?"

"That's it. It's *Escherichia coli*, but scientists abbreviate it." His mouth quirked. "Like *T. rex*. *E. coli* is just a normal bug found in the gut of almost all mammals, most vertebrates. It's fecal bacteria because you find it in shit. Researchers love the bug because it's ubiquitous, reproduces quickly, is hard to kill accidentally, and it grows in just about any medium. It's a large cell, too, easy to isolate."

His voice had risen with his enthusiasm. The waitress brought our sandwiches and drinks, another cup of coffee for me, water for him, and he grew quiet again. I prodded him: "You talk like a science major."

"Because that's what I am. I've taken my time about it, burned out once, then started back to grad school. I'm ABD now at UVM, microbiology." Reading my inquisitive look, he explained, "All But Dissertation. Just shy of a PhD. Of course, that means I've got work to do. I thought I'd have the degree by now, but my advisor kept quibbling with my proposal. He thought he knew more about my subject than I did." He took a bite of his sandwich. "He didn't," he said, the words muffled.

"That stopped your progress to the degree?"

"You could say so. But Dr. Summers died last summer. I'll probably sign up for a new advisor next fall and finally finish up." He sipped his water. "Anyway, *E. coli* has been around throughout human history. Our meat animals have it in their guts, because it helps them to break down and digest nutrients. Now something weird has happened in the last twenty years. It's started to kill people."

"Mind if I ask you a question?"

He shrugged.

"What the hell kind of sandwich is that?"

He looked at it in surprise. "Tofu Reuben."

"You're joking."

"No, Donna—the waitress—knows it's my standard order. Lots of people in this town are vegetarians. You can substitute tofu for any meat on the menu."

"Sounds like my kind of town," I said.

Jerry munched his mock Reuben. "Anyhow, let me tell you about the change in *E. coli*. Bacteria can mutate quickly. They change their genes in response to their environment. A hundred thousand generations of bacteria can grow during the lifespan of a single cow, and the bugs evolve much faster than we do. Well, in terms of generations it may be similar, but in real time, it's much shorter."

He waggled part of his sandwich at me. "Now, as the bacteria adapt, they rewrite their genetic code, see? The bits of DNA rearrange to give new blueprints. In the 1960s and '70s, dairymen began putting antibiotics into cattle feed to prevent diseases like mastitis. It worked great. Cows thrived, lived longer, fattened faster, produced more milk. By the '80s practically every milk cow in the country got antibiotics in her feed.

"But the antibiotics were changing the *E. coli*, killing off the weaker strains. The stronger ones mutated new defenses against the antibiotics. I don't mean it was a conscious thing. Bacteria don't think. But millions of mutations happen all the time. Almost all are bad ones and the bacteria die. But when a useful mutation does occur, that gives the mutated organism an edge and it grows like crazy, taking the place of the others that are weakened or killed. Clear so far?"

"Darwin 101," I said.

"Right. Now, one of the mutated strains, *E. coli* 0157:H7, changed in a way that made it not only more resistant to antibiotics but that also caused it to produce toxins as part of its metabolism. Bacteria eat and poop just like we do, and the poop from this little bugger causes people to get diarrhea, headaches, high fever, kidney failure, blood poisoning. It kills people."

"That's the one that causes the food recalls?"

"Yeah, meat and any other food that gets contaminated because cows are in the area. Fruit juices have been contaminated with it, unpasteurized milk, lots of stuff. It's actually all over the place in the food processing industry now."

"All that because people fed antibiotics to cattle?"

"Hard to say for certain, but that's the most likely reason. But what's really cool is that if you introduce that mutated strain of *E. coli* into a medium with other strains, the genetic material from the mutant can jump into the others. They quickly become just as virulent. The jump actually comes from even smaller parasites, a type of virus that infects bacteria and nothing else."

"'Great fleas have little fleas upon their backs to bite 'em,'" I quoted. "'And little fleas have lesser fleas, and so ad infinitum.'"

"Heard it," said Jerry, unimpressed, pushing away his empty plate. "Anyway, the parasites, the viruses, are called bacteriophages. They can carry the genes from one bacterium to all the others." He spread his fingers. "Imagine that Superman was real. He comes along, shakes your hand, and instead of catching the common cold from him, you discover you can fly and bullets bounce off you. That's how dramatic the change is. It happens all the time in nature, especially with bacteria and fungi."

"So there're more and more nasty diseases loose in the world."

"More and more that are resistant to antibiotics."

"All right. What in the world does this have to do with Caleb Benson?"

"I have no earthly idea. If Grandpa was talking about that, he was off on some wild goose chase of his own. Benson has nothing to do with cattle."

"He has a lot to do with timber. Do genes jump in forests?"

"Unlikely to be significant. Trees grow so slowly, not like a bacterium."

"Other plants?"

"Look, go to the newspaper office and ask them to dig up the story I did on this three years ago. But in a nutshell, back in the '70s scientists figured out how to recode DNA without hybridization, without crossbreeding. We could simply extract it, recode it, and then insert it in a plant or animal. Even take genes from one life form and put them into a totally different one. Use a virus, or just inject it with something called a gene gun."

"Genetic engineering."

"Right. Say there's a gene that controls the fertility of a seed. If a scientist can turn that gene off, the plant is sterile.

If he could go a step further and figure out how to set that gene so its normal state is off but it can turn on if you feed the plant a certain chemical, one your company manufactured and patented, then you could control the fertility of a crop plant."

"I've read of something called Terminator Seeds."

"Yeah, it's more complex than that, but in the same arena. It's a way of making sure farmers can't use seeds unless they buy from you, because only you have the chemical to make the seeds fertile."

"Didn't the government stop that?"

"Put it on hold. Too much publicity, and scientists were concerned about the gene jumping into the wild by crosspollination. One company put a gene into soybeans and corn to make the plants resistant to their herbicide, so farmers could spray and kill the weeds without killing the crops. But the gene jumped from the food crops into weeds that were closely enough related to react to soybean and corn pollen. The result was superweeds, created accidentally, the same way we created a virulent kind of E. coli accidentally."

"But if a plant can fight off a chemical, that just makes it stronger," I said. "I don't see how that can endanger a forest. Could a forest be taken over by superweeds?"

"No," he said flatly. "I can't imagine any kind of genetic engineering that would endanger a forest." His enthusiasm had ebbed. He turned and beckoned the waitress. She came over with an empty coffee cup and a small metal pot of steaming water. Jerry took a plastic bag from his shirt pocket and dumped some brown dust into his cup. It had a strange, musty smell. He poured the hot water on it. "My tonic," he said. "Helps the digestion, good for the blood."

"Herbs?"

"And Chinese mushrooms." He stirred and sipped the tea, rolling it in his mouth as though it were a fine wine before swallowing. "Want to try some?"

"I'll pass, thanks."

"Most people are afraid to try something new." He took another appreciative drink. "OK, back to genetic engineering. Here's something I'm researching, getting ready to write about. Last year a company found the gene that controls how fast grasses grow. They found a way to flip its switch so grass will slow down to grow at approximately one-tenth its normal rate. Now they can sell you grass seed that will grow so slowly that you only need to mow twice a season."

"Sounds ideal for golf courses."

"But if it jumps, then the weed grasses that control erosion, that provide food for rabbits and deer, grow one-tenth as fast as they should, and a whole ecosystem is thrown out of balance. Worse, wheat, rice, rye, barley, oats, all these are related to the grass on your lawn. Most food grains are overbred, overweight grass seeds. If their growth slowed, the seeds wouldn't mature and the world would starve. Half the food in the world comes directly from grass seeds—we call them grains—or indirectly, from animals fed on those seeds."

"And what's being done about that?"

"It's being debated, but the whole system is so interbred that nothing much can be done politically. Here in Vermont, everyone's flipped out because so many dairy farms use rBGH, a synthetic growth hormone that contributes to milk production. Now, the *r* in rBGH stands for 'recombinant,' meaning it's genetically engineered. BGH is 'bovine growth hormone.' It makes cows grow faster. The human equivalent determines whether a fetus becomes a dwarf or a seven-foot-tall NBA star."

"Does the bovine version affect humans?"

"Government says no, but some researchers and scientists, especially in Europe, disagree. They have real concerns it may be linked to breast cancer or other types of hormone-mediated cancers."

"Has that been proven?"

"No. Human studies are difficult. You can't just give a group of women rBGH and see if they get cancer. That's illegal and unethical—unless you arrange to drop it into their food or water supply and follow it for thirty years to see what happens. We did that with DDT, and effectively we're doing it now with rBGH."

He moved his cup around on the table as if he were playing with a model car. "Vermont now has the second highest breast cancer rate in the United States." He laughed, a bitter sound that reminded me Jeremiah's daughter had died of cancer. "Could be coincidence, they say."

"And Vermonters know that?"

"Sure, it's been in the papers. That's why organic farmers want to label their milk as rBGH-free, why Ben and Jerry wanted to label their products the same way. But close to twenty-five years ago now the FDA rode into town and wrote up a policy. Now if you mention rBGH at all on your label, you have to say something nice about it, like it's the same as natural hormones. And you can't say anything negative about it, or even question the whole idea of hormone-spiked cows."

"Speak no ill of big business."

"And this is among the biggest. Over half the food crops in the US are now genetically modified. Practically all the domestic beef and chicken are laced with hormones, pesticides, antibiotics. It's an unholy mess, and the government won't do a damn thing about it because they don't represent the people but the corporations that pay for their junkets and finance their campaigns. That's all in my article in the paper."

"So. Do you think your grandfather's death was engineered by a big company?"

Jerry shook his head. "I don't see a connection. As far as I'm concerned, this is just stuff I like to write about. And Grandpa seemed interested in it."

"And not long ago Jeremiah was upset about Caleb Benson and talking about gene-jumping."

"I really don't think there's anything there," Jerry said, again in that depressed, listless voice. "Grandpa just had a burr under his saddle, that's all. I can't see how any of this could've had anything to do with the car that hit him." He sighed. "I might as well tell you, this morning I called Benson's business to ask if they knew anything about Grandpa contacting Benson. I got passed around to a PR man who said he didn't know what I was talking about, and that was that." He flicked a finger at the very small remnant of his sandwich he hadn't finished. "Odds are the soy that this tofu is made from is genetically modified. Almost all American soy is."

"But no forests."

He shook his head. "No forests. Trees take too long to grow. Companies are interested in this year's profits, not some potential gain in thirty years."

"So what did the two guys who tied you to the tree want to discuss?"

"Thanks for lunch." He reached for his jacket.

"You still want to pretend it never happened."

"Nothing happened. Don't bring it up again. If you think you're working for me or my grandfather because some of this stuff happened around you, you're not. I hereby officially fire you, as the representative of the estate. Stay out of my life, OK?"

"Calm down, cowboy."

"Don't patronize me. I don't need you to save me from anybody. There's nothing I can't handle. You're off this case, got it?"

I pulled one of Jeremiah's twenties from my pocket and dropped it on the table. "Jerry, it's crystal clear. But just one thing: even if I was willing to work for you—you couldn't afford it."

He turned and walked away. I picked up the envelope and pulled out Jerry's article to learn more about gene-jumping and Superman. At the moment, I felt low on invulnerability.

15

Jerry told it better than he wrote it, I thought as I considered my next move. I didn't know enough about Caleb Benson. He said old Jeremiah hadn't feared him, but feared change. Personally I wasn't too happy with the kind of change that turned a benign, useful bug into a killer bacterium, and wondered if Benson had wandered from lumber into cattle or something that might involve bugs that Benson's associate Frank would make sure were killed off. I wanted to find out if Benson's enterprises might have anything to do with gene-jumping.

It did not take the skills of a licensed PI to find Benson's house. I asked a random person on the street and got precise directions. It wasn't the kind of place you'd expect a man of Benson's attainments to occupy, but it was substantial, an older house that at second glance had undergone more face-lifts than the average TV talk show host. As I walked up and rang the bell, two wall-mounted video cameras eyed me.

A blonde woman, probably the third wife that Jerry had mentioned, answered the door. She wore a gray wool sweater and tan slacks and let me into a foyer that somehow reminded me of a small display room in a museum. I introduced myself and asked if I could see Mr. Benson. She gave me a mildly shocked look. "Oh, he's not home. He's at his office in Newport."

"It's hard to catch him there without an appointment," I said. "What time will he be back?"

The question seemed to offend her. She reopened the front door, crafted of antique walnut and cut-glass. It was probably worth more than my whole cabin. "I'm not his secretary."

"Are you his wife?"

The sun slanted in through the open door. She replied oddly: "He's my husband." She had good coloring, a baby-doll sort of face, but I could see that in ten years she might run to flesh.

I said, "Then you're Eva." The name had appeared in the newspaper story of the confrontation Benson had been involved in, though the photo showed only him, not his wife.

"I'm Eva. And you're Mr. Tyler, and whatever you want with my husband, he isn't here."

"What I want is to talk to him for a minute about Jeremiah Smith."

She closed the door, and we stood in the foyer facing each other. Behind her a grandfather clock taller than she was clacked off the seconds. "Jeremiah Smith?" she asked, her blue eyes showing surprise. "The old man who—that accident?"

"That's him."

"But he's dead." Her lips, which she had colored with some kind of cantaloupe-colored gloss, compressed. "He was walking beside the highway and a car hit him. Sad." She blinked twice, rapidly. "Why do you want to talk to my husband about Mr. Smith? I hardly think they knew each other, and if you're thinking my husband was the one who hit him—"

I shook my head. "I'd prefer to ask him the questions, Eva."

"Then it's not a business matter."

I shrugged and took a wild shot. "I do have an interest in forestry and genetics. So did Jeremiah. Someone thought our interests might have something in common with Mr. Benson's companies."

"Who?"

"Jeremiah's grandson, Jerry."

Eva Benson blushed and half turned, blurting, "But Caleb—" and then she recovered and took a deep breath, as calm as a professional actor. "I know Jerry. We were in high school together."

"Oh, you were friends?"

"No, he was two grades ahead of me." She seemed on the verge of saying something else, but then gave me a patronizing smile. "I'll tell my husband you called, Mr. Tyler. Do you have a card?"

"No. If I can't find Mr. Benson in Newport, I'll just stop by again later."

She gave me a level look. "I don't know that you'll have much luck. He's rarely home." Her eyebrows raised as if she were asking a question. But she didn't put it in words, and when she opened the door again, I left her in the big house. She closed the door slowly, so that all the way down the front walk I felt her gaze on my back. The door clicked as I reached the sidewalk.

I walked the three blocks from the Benson house back to Main Street. Montpelier hadn't had snow in two or three days, and the sidewalks were dry, though patches of dirty snow lay in strips along the shady sides of curbs. The town strings up tinsel and a giant fairy-light snowflake for First Night, and the decorations were still up, quivering in the breeze. I supposed they would be in place until spring.

In an investigation it's always good to look for loose ends, and now I had a small one. When Jerry Smith had told me about his grandfather's driving him out to the Benson place, he'd made it sound as if he didn't know Eva at all. That fact, and the way she'd reacted when I'd mentioned Jerry's name, made me wonder exactly how well they had known each other. Jerry had insisted that Benson had nothing to do with a couple of guys tying him to a tree and zapping him with several thousand volts of electricity. Eva Benson had impulsively mentioned her husband's name when I brought up Jerry. It was enough to make me wonder.

I got into my Jeep, parked at a curb midway between the diner and the newspaper building, and pondered. There is such a thing as pareidolia, the human tendency to see coherent figures in random shapes: New Hampshire's Old Man of the Mountain, a profile in granite, the Madonna in the scorch patterns of a toasted sandwich, a cloud that is very like a whale. I had to consider the possibility that everything that had happened was random, that there was no real pattern. Somebody putting a wick in Jeremiah's gas tank and shooting at us might be unrelated to anything else, a crackpot, a warped redneck prankster. Jerry's abduction might have been done by two guys who had no connection to the truck burning. Jeremiah could have been hit by a tourist bleary after too many hours behind the wheel. Genes might have nothing to do with anything.

But Sylvia had told me the car had deliberately swerved to hit Jeremiah. And her lesson in the forest, if that's what it was, seemed to tell me to look for unity in apparent chaos, for the pattern in randomness, and for something that was a danger to all life on earth, a pretty damn grandiose notion. What common factors did I have? The strongest was Jerry himself. And then Bill Grinder, who popped up in odd places at odd times.

I weighed the probable success of a trip to Newport. I had no leverage to force open Benson's office door. On the other hand, the newspaper office was half a block away. I left the envelope of articles in the car and went to see if Gina or anybody else there had any new ideas.

It was still early afternoon, but two of the three staff members I'd met had left the office. Only Gina Berkof was there, sitting at her desk and rattling her keyboard again. I walked across the echoing, open room and sat in the old wooden chair beside her desk.

She hit the Enter key and said, "That's the big problem with not having a private office. I can't close the door."

"Sorry to bother you again. Thanks for the copies of the stories."

"No problem. Now what can I tell you?" She swiveled toward me and picked up her blue pencil, as though she felt more at ease that way.

"Little more information. Eva Benson?"

"Oh, boy," she said. "Look, this is a newspaper. We have no interest in rumors."

"What rumors?"

"Ask the woman. She'll probably talk to you. If the rumors are true." Gina lifted an eyebrow and smiled.

"At least tell me if she has any involvement with her husband's business interests."

"I don't know."

"And are either of them involved with the Abenaki?"

She dropped the pencil. "What? Listen, did Jerry tell you about—" Then she said, "No, he wouldn't have. He doesn't know. OK, have you been checking up on me or was that a lucky shot?"

"I haven't been checking on you."

She said, "Because the Abenaki cause is kind of a hot button with me. I'm working on an article. The Abenaki got a royal screwing from the state, and from the federal government for that matter. All they want is recognition that they're an actual tribe, but the state claims they don't exist, that all the Abenaki were exterminated. That ignores the Abenaki who show up living and breathing, with birth lineages and family history and all that. The state seems to claim that the Abenaki can't still be around because Vermont was just so damned good at genocide."

"What's at stake?"

"What's always at stake?" Gina asked. "Money, of course. There's a core of state politicians who are afraid that if they grant the Abenaki claims, then the tribe will demand some of their land back to create a reservation. That will cut into the tax base, complicate land claims, stir things up. Better to keep them dead Indians."

"So the Abenaki have staked a claim to land?"

"No, no, not that I've heard. At this point they just want the existence of their people to be formally acknowledged."

"Benson is a big landowner."

"Yeah, raw land up north, some right around here, too, but if you think he'd be involved in this because he's afraid of losing his land, think again. If the state did recognize any Abenaki claims to Benson's land, they'd compensate him."

I looked at the pencil on the scarred wooden top of her desk. "But in eminent domain cases, when the state takes someone's land, the state itself decides on the price to pay for it. That might not be the same valuation that Benson would put on the land."

"Well, at this point it's all academic. The Abenaki haven't made any claim. And besides, Benson is politically well connected enough that he'd be sure to be handsomely compensated, even if smaller land owners got screwed."

I was following the train of thought: "Might there be a possibility, though? Any Abenaki remains, any old Indian graveyards in Vermont?"

"Oh, sure, lots of them. I know of one case in which a burial site has been protected by the government, but really, I don't think that Benson, or his wife, or Jerry have any connection with this Abenaki business." She gave me a speculative look. "Wait a minute. Jeremiah Smith's wife was part Indian, wasn't she? Was she an Abenaki?"

Reporters had the pareidolia bug, too. "That's right," I said. Then after a pause, I added, "And I've met a woman who looks like a Native American, wears buckskin clothes and moccasins. She showed up at my cabin outside of Northfield. I'd guess her to be in her late twenties, early thirties, black hair, big dark brown eyes. Her name is Sylvia. Know her?"

Gina shook her head. "No. I might ask some of my Abenaki contacts, but she doesn't sound like anyone I know. Is she related to Jeremiah's wife? Was Jeremiah's death really accidental, or was he killed because somebody didn't like his Abenaki connections?"

"I don't know. What do you think?"

"I didn't know Smith well. I met him only a few times, but my reading of him was that he was totally nonpolitical, not like his grandson. Jeremiah's passion was trees, not Native Americans. With the exception of his wife."

"OK," I said. "Try this one: Do you know a kid in his early twenties, blond, tall, skinny, prominent Adam's apple, a guy who works for Bill Grinder in Northfield? His name's Darryl."

"Oh, boy," she said. "Look, it's a small place, but not that small. No, I don't know anything about a Darryl who works for

Bill Grinder. I have work to do, Mr. Tyler. If you can nail the bastard who hit poor old Jeremiah and didn't even stop, good for you. But I'll tell you, it seems to me you're trying to build it into some kind of conspiracy. I'm no expert, but I'd say you need to look for a car with a dent in its fender, not for Abenaki in the woodpile and little blonde wives thirty years younger than their husbands."

"All right. But please do me one last favor. I'd like you to call the police department and check on something. Might even be a story in it."

"Manipulator." But she reached for her phone. With her hand on the instrument, she said, "Why don't you do it?"

"They didn't want me to involve myself with the case, and I don't want to draw their attention." I then told the lie: "I have a witness who says there was a suspicious car in the area around the time Jeremiah was hit. It showed up later near town here, a dark Subaru wagon, apparently driven by a drunk. I know the police got a tip on it and were looking for it. If they found it, I'd like to know whose car it was. Police records are public. They should tell you."

"But remember, we don't do crime news." She took her hand off the phone. "All right, I know someone on the force, and I'll put in a call to him, but he won't be on shift until late this afternoon. I'll call you if there's anything. Right now I really have to get back to work. We're right up to deadline. In fact, half my staff is now at the printer's, having the plates for section one shot."

I jotted down my cell number for her. She had already opened a file on her computer and was assaulting the keyboard. I wished her a good afternoon. She grunted around the blue pencil, which she now had clenched sideways in her teeth.

16

Newport is sixty-odd miles north of Montpelier, located at the south tip of Lake Memphremagog. There is a spot where the lake pinches off a bay. On the east shore is a country club. On the west shore is an unpretentious brick building, modern but drab, that houses the main office of Benson Consolidated Inc.

Benson was not on the premises, I was told. He currently was surveying some part of his land by helicopter. He was not expected back. I left my phone number.

With Benson unreachable, I thought I might try finding Darryl. Grinder had seemed oddly protective of the kid. There was a possibility that Darryl was another loose end, so I drove back to Northfield to check it out.

The social center of Northfield is a blinking stoplight in the middle of town. Nearby is a small park that boasts a statue, and at the far end of the park is an old train station, now converted into a library. Running along either side of the park are storefronts dating back to the nineteenth century, none still occupied by original businesses. A hardware store, a pizzeria, the phone company, a moribund travel agency, and a drugstore constitute the major enterprises, all but the phone company locally owned.

Opposite the park and the main commercial district, on the other side of Main Street, there's another strip of old buildings with similar businesses housed in them, a barber, a bank, a deli, a florist, a bookstore, an antique shop, and a realtor. Just around the corner is the police station, located conveniently across the street from a doughnut shop.

At the four corners close by the Northfield police station, Delilah's Café faces the park diagonally. It's a standard American menu. Wanda works weekdays while her daughter is in school, and on the two busier afternoons she pulls a longer shift, so as to have weekends free.

I walked in to the strains of Johnny Paycheck singing "Take this Job and Shove It" on the jukebox that never seemed to acquire any tunes from this century. It was late for lunch, a little early for dinner.

Eight men dressed in hunting gear and army surplus sat at a table and booth in the back, swapping stories and raucous laughter. A young couple sat in one of the other four booths along the wall with the two small windows, blinds slatted to ward off the western sunlight. Right behind them a woman in a red business suit sat opposite a middle-aged couple, a three-ring binder with real estate photos and descriptions open on the table. A solitary old man sat at the counter, reading a paper and nursing a cup of coffee.

Wanda, on counter duty, gave me an unreadable glance before vanishing into the kitchen in the back. I sat on the stool at the end of the counter nearest the door and cash register. Debby, the pleasant middle-aged woman who owns the place, asked, "What'll it be, Oakley?"

It had been nearly four hours since lunch with Jerry. "BLT," I said. "But make it a CLT, cheese instead of bacon."

She squinted. "Cheese sandwich, lettuce and tomato. Here or to go?"

"Here if you can get Wanda to come out and talk to me."

"I'm not sure I can do that. What kind of cheese, Cheddar, Swiss, or American?"

"Cheddar, extra sharp. And a Coke, no ice."

Debby called the order back, then stood in the doorway to the kitchen and said something in a voice too soft for me to catch. She went on over to freshen up cups among the hunting party in the back.

After a minute Wanda brought out a tray laden with burgers and sodas. She took them to the realtor and her clients. Watching her walk, I remembered what it had been like to hold her and felt a twinge of loss.

The first time I'd seen her had been late the previous summer, the week after I moved into the cabin. I'd needed some hardware and had come into town for it, then stopped at the café for lunch. Wanda served me. She's what John Lincoln always kidded me about, one of my skinny little blondes. She thought her ears stuck out and covered them with a poufy hairdo that made her face look wide across the cheekbones. We flirted a little that first day, and the next time I came in, this time for breakfast, I'd asked her out.

Wanda said she wanted to go bowling, of all things. She had bowled in high school, but not since. She held a BA degree and was a year into a master's program in English literature when she got pregnant and dropped out to find a job and be a mom. She still dreamed of eventually teaching English.

She wasn't a great bowler, and I wasn't much better, but we rolled balls down the thundering lanes, drank beers, and talked. She told me she'd thrown her boyfriend out the day before I first met her. He was, it seemed, a no good son of a bitch who didn't care enough about his future to hold a job.

At some point Wanda managed to bowl a strike, and I kissed her. She responded. We didn't even finish the game. Part of me knew how stupid it all was, shooting fish in a barrel. Wanda told me to drive her home, told me her daughter was away, spending a week with her grandparents down in Brattle-boro. Instead of taking Wanda directly home, I drove to my cabin. We fell into bed and she clung to me through the night.

I told myself that the evening was therapy for her, for me, a little bit of mutual fun that left us both feeling better. No harm done.

I shouldn't lie to myself. The next morning Wanda was broody, accusatory, telling me I'd taken advantage of her after plying her with four beers. She didn't normally drink that much, she didn't sleep around, she wasn't a loose woman. I began to suspect that her problems with the husband and the boyfriend were not as one-sided as I'd heard. I found myself not liking her as much, and when I dropped her off at her house later, we behaved with icy formality. It took another couple of weeks for me to realize we had both been acting like victims. That made us good Americans, I supposed. We talked, now and then, when I saw her on the street or came into the café, but I still had made no apologies, mended no fences.

She finished with the testosterone crew, vanished again into the kitchen, and came out with my sandwich. Her mouth was tight as she brought me the cola and CLT.

"Here," she said. "What do you want to talk about?"

She wore no makeup, but she didn't need it. She had one of those fresh faces that was attractive enough without window dressing.

"It's been months," I said. "Can't we be friendly?"

She frowned. "It's hard for me to forgive myself. I was stupid."

"For what it's worth, I'm sorry," I said. "I took advantage of you. That was wrong."

Then she gave me a rueful smile. "I don't hold a grudge. But I do hold a job. You've got maybe five minutes before I have to make the rounds again."

"How's things at home?"

"Fine, now that Darryl's out of our lives."

I paused with my sandwich halfway to my mouth. "Darryl?"

"I told you about him, way last summer. I kicked him out, remember?"

"I don't think you told me his name back then. Is he a tall guy, blond?"

"Yes. He's never finished a thing in his life, including school. He wanted to get back together with me last fall, but I've had enough of him."

"I think he showed up at my place this morning, armed with a rifle."

"I'll be back." Wanda went around the room leaving checks, freshening drinks, and then returned to me. "Darryl came after you with a rifle?" she asked in a low voice. "You're not kidding me?"

"He had a rifle. He didn't exactly threaten me. Do you know where he's been, where he was last night or this morning?"

"I don't keep tabs on him, and I haven't even seen him in a week or more. Look, I don't want to talk about that bastard."

"OK. It's good to see you again. Did you by any chance tell Darryl about us?"

"I don't tell Darryl anything, and I don't want to talk about him. Do you have any other subject in mind?"

"How about us?"

That was the wrong thing to say. A new customer came in and sat down at the counter. Wanda leaned forward and said shortly, "Ask Darryl about Darryl. Read about me in the papers." She went to wait on the new guy.

I finished my sandwich in ten minutes. Wanda acted as if I had become invisible. Neither she nor Debby brought me the bill, but I left the cost of the sandwich plus a three-dollar tip on the counter. Wanda came to collect it and muttered, "Thanks."

The jukebox was playing Leonard Cohen's "Tower of Song." I said, "Look, can't we start over? I mean, just as friends?"

"Maybe some time. Not now."

The old man with the paper was watching us. "I'll be around," I said.

Darryl and Wanda. A possible reason for Darryl to hold a grudge against me. Patterns in chaos.

I crossed the intersection and went into the Backwoods Bookshop, a store that buys and sells used books, DVDs, and computer games. They also have three shelves of new books, a few bestsellers, a lot of religious, gardening, and hunting titles. Bernie, the owner, usually sits behind a cluttered desk at the front, reading and chain-smoking. Bernie is in his late fifties with pink skin, a thin white beard, and longish hair. I'd guess his weight as somewhere between two seventy-five and three hundred. He looked up as I came in, making the bell above the door tinkle. "How ya doin'?" His voice had the rasp of a long-time smoker.

"Fine, Bernie. How are you?"

"Got the goddam gout, can you imagine? I'm getting old. Gout!" He took a deep drag on a filter cigarette.

I browsed the NEW ARRIVALS table—the NEW meaning they were new to Backwoods Bookshop, not to the world. In a pile of hardcovers I picked up an oddity, a book from the '50s called *Inside the Space Ships* by George Adamski. It was a true-life UFO adventure, complete with actual photos of pie plates in the sky.

"Helluva book, that one," said Bernie, whose eyesight was still keen. "Read that when I was a kid. I tell you, it changed my life."

"Ever been abducted?" I asked him.

"In my dreams." He chuckled. "Adamski seems pretty damn foolish now, but hey, the book got me interested in science and hooked on reading. Say, if you're interested, I got in two copies of *L.A. P.I.*, found them on the Internet. Here ya go. One's a library copy, the other a good first edition."

I picked up the good first edition of the bad book written by a hack, basing it on the lousy screenplay from the movie they'd made about John Lincoln solving the case of a kidnapped California senator's daughter. The movie itself was creaky with age, twenty-five years old or more now. Lincoln hadn't written the screenplay or even had any opportunity to comment on the script, but he had suffered. The movie made California law enforcement out to be totally venal and corrupt—and inept and incompetent.

After it came out, Lincoln began to be regularly stopped, ticketed, and once even arrested: changing lanes without using turn signals, having a minute crack in a taillight lens, parking an inch and a half too far from a curb. In disgust, he'd packed it in and moved to Atlanta, where a major airline had some security issues they'd wanted his advice on, and there I'd met him ten years ago. John didn't like the movie, didn't like to be reminded of it.

"It's lousy," I told Bernie.

"True story, though," Bernie replied.

"Only in the sense that some people with those names lived in California at the time. John didn't save the attorney general from assassination. Half the information the book has him turning up came from stuff he'd read in the papers."

"Yeah, but it reads well."

"Maybe if you like dime-store detective stories."

"Yeah, actually I do."

"Then it's your sort of thing. Hey, Bernie, do you by any chance know a tall blond kid in town named Darryl?"

He stubbed out his cigarette in an overflowing ash tray. "Guy that lived with Wanda for about six weeks? You and her making up?"

"This isn't about Wanda. This morning Bill Grinder and a kid named Darryl came onto my property, rabbit hunting they said, and I chased them off."

"Yeah, that'd be the same Darryl. He works for Bill now and then, when he feels like it or needs some cash. See, what you need to do is register and post your land—"

"I know."

"So do it. You can't fight the system. Hunting's big business around here, draws in eighty-odd thousand people every November. Tourist hunters, bringing money. Tell you, though, those out-of-state yahoos are a pain in the ass, raising hell, trashing the place, shooting people's dogs and cows."

"You don't hunt, I take it."

He lit a cigarette. "Hunted Charlie in Vietnam. Had enough of toting a rifle to last me the rest of my life. I don't like the taste of venison, and killing just for fun is sick." He blew out a cloud of smoke. "You ever kill anybody in your line of work?"

"That's classified," I said, and he wheezed out a laugh. "Tell me about Darryl."

"Killing is a hard thing," Bernie said as though he hadn't heard me. "I got to return to the world thirty years ago next year, and I still wake up in the middle of the night thinking I'm in the jungle and Charlie's just ahead."

"Tell me about Darryl," I prompted again.

Bernie coughed. "Darryl grew up in the Northeast Kingdom. You know where that is?"

"I know." The Northeast Kingdom was a nickname for three counties of Vermont, and it had been dreamed up by US senator George Aiken around 1950. It's border country, hard up against Canada.

"OK," Bernie said. "When Darryl was a teenager his mama moved down here. She'd broken up with his old man. That was Billy Garret, a mean son of a bitch, doubly mean when he was drinking. Last I heard, he's in prison for dropping a tree with a chainsaw. It landed on a guy's house, nearly killed the man's wife. They charged him with attempted homicide. He had a grudge against the guy over some stupid shit, money owed or money borrowed." Bernie paused to feed his nicotine habit and then added, "Billy was bound for prison, one way or the other. He used to beat the shit out of Darryl and his brothers."

"Brothers?"

He nodded through the streamers of blue smoke. "Three boys, Darryl the youngest. Other two left home before Darryl and his mama moved to town. I don't know much about them. Both of them out of state, so far as I know. Now, mind, I don't know Darryl personally. He never comes into the store. I don't think he's the kind of person who likes to read."

"Bill Grinder ever come in?"

"No. I've spoken with him. They say he's a good mechanic, but he's no reader, either."

"How about Jerry Smith?"

"The college boy that writes for *This Week?* Yeah, he was in town a lot because of his grandpa. I special ordered some science books for him, pretty damn expensive—wait a minute, his grandpa was Jeremiah Smith, the old guy who got hit by the car. You investigating that?"

I grinned. "I could tell you, Bernie, but then I'd have to kill you."

He laughed so hard that his body jiggled, and then he started to cough. He gasped, "I get it. You're looking into the hit-and-run but you don't want to make a big issue of it. So why all the questions? What's the connection between Grinder, Garret, and Jeremiah?"

"I don't have evidence of any connection. Anybody else ask you about any of them?"

"No."

"I wouldn't say a lot about them if anyone does. I wouldn't even hint that anybody at all in town could be linked to such an unfortunate death."

"Gotcha," Bernie said.

"How about a Native American woman named Sylvia? Know her? She lives somewhere around here." I described her.

Bernie shook his head long before I finished the description. "Never heard of her, and a woman like that would be noticed around here. Sorry." He gave a couple of final coughs. "Now, I knew old Jeremiah. He'd drop in and shoot the breeze, buy a book once in a while. Most of his book shopping, though, he did in Montpelier. And I'd see him now and again leaving the library with a stack of books a foot high."

"Did he ever say anything to you about Caleb Benson?"

"Jesus on a pogo stick! Those two are about as different as two men could get."

"Did Benson grow up around here?"

"He was another Northeast Kingdom boy. He was only around during the summers, and those he spent in Montpelier. I'm a little older than he is. His parents shipped him off to three or four different prep schools, but he usually managed to get himself expelled. Smart kid. Mean as hell, though. Money ruined him. His parents had so much of it, he was immune." He stubbed out his latest cigarette and reached for another, but paused before lighting it with his Zippo. "Tell you what, Benson's smart and he's rich. You don't want him for an enemy."

"How did Jeremiah feel about him?"

Bernie got the cigarette going. "Hell, Jeremiah didn't care who liked him, who didn't." He frowned out the window as a woman walked past and then said, "Jeremiah kind of thought of himself as a one-man forestry police force. Over the years he's made trouble for two dozen loggers or more. He caught them skidding logs across creeks, clear-cutting a stand without a permit, stuff like that, usually in remote areas where they figure nobody will notice or bother with them. But he was always out patrolling the woods."

"Benson's in the timber business. He owns a big spread of land."

"Yeah, but he's no logger. He hires that done. I never heard he had any kind of run-in with Jeremiah."

"Or Jerry?"

"Couldn't tell you. Benson supports politicians, Smith writes about politics. They're of opposite persuasions, but I don't' know of any feud."

"Seen anybody driving with out-of-state plates?"

"I don't drive. Walk from here to home and back. You don't notice license plates so much when you're on foot. You want to take one of those books on John Lincoln off my hands?"

"No thanks, I have a copy already."

He went back to his book, but said, "You might not know, but Wanda and her daughter have been living all on their own since the night she went bowling with you. She's not seeing anybody."

"Thanks," I said, opening the door. No secrets in a small town, none at all.

With a possible exception for murder.

17

My Jeep was parked outside the pharmacy. I sat in it and called Information on my cell phone. Though 411 had a listing for Darryl Garret, when I dialed the number I got his recorded voice telling me to leave a message. I didn't.

It was almost closing time. I walked to the phone company and asked if I could see a directory. The receptionist looked surprised, but gave me one and told me to keep it. I found Darryl's address, a number on High Street, a paved street that runs from downtown and becomes a county route along the crest of a ridge overlooking the town. I went back and tossed the phone book into the back seat of the Jeep.

I could smell wood smoke on the afternoon air, air that was coppery fresh from having crossed two thousand miles of Arctic tundra and Canadian forests. They'll tell you in Vermont that lately the winters have been mild, the growing season longer, hard on cold-weather plants that now mature too early, rough on hibernating animals. But the heart of winter is still cold, and the crispness of a fading Vermont day reminds me that I'm alive.

I drove to Bill Grinder's place. The afternoon had become warm enough so that the streets streamed with meltwater from the heaps of snow scraped to the sides. Grinder's garage looked busy: a dozen cars clustered around it, and his new tow truck was parked almost as far back as his house. I went in through the office, which smelled of oil and gas, and found it empty. I heard Grinder's voice from the garage bays and found him there yelling at a young man who held a pneumatic lug wrench as though it were a weapon. Grinder was red in the face, spraying spittle and gesturing with a cigar butt. "Goddam, you flip one more bolt like that and hit the paint job on this car, I'll dock you a week's pay!"

"I didn't mean to do it!" The young mechanic looked like a high school junior or senior, with long brown hair pulled back in a ponytail and a blotch of acne on his cheeks. His posture and tone reminded me of a whipped dog.

Grinder caught sight of me. "Now what the hell do you want?" he demanded of me, his voice a snarl. He wasn't in hunting togs now, but green work pants and a long-sleeved thermal T shirt. Red and white striped suspenders held the pants up.

I approached him as the kid scuttled around the Lexus. "I'm looking for Darryl."

"You got a hell of a nerve! Take up with his girlfriend so she dumps him, then you run out on her. If I was Darryl, I'd kick your worthless ass."

"That happened months ago. This isn't about that."

"So you gonna post your land, you warnin' him off?"

Across the back of the bay stood a bank of computerized diagnostic equipment, shiny and new, spread out and looking expensive. "Maybe I don't need to talk to him if you tell me what you and he are doing for Caleb Benson."

Grinder took three quick steps to the wall and grabbed a tire iron. He came toward me with it over his shoulder, squinting one eye like the old spinach fancier. "This is private property. I got a right to defend myself. Davey will swear he heard you threaten me."

Davey, the kid with the ponytail, stared at us over the hood of the Lexus.

Grinder didn't attack, but he growled, "Get the hell out of here or I'll break your skull open."

He'd given me the answer, so I left. In the level light of sunset, I drove to High Street and followed it out of town, watching the numbers. The pavement was beaten all to hell by the weather.

The change in Grinder troubled me. He and Jeremiah had seemed amicable enough, but since Jeremiah's death something had curdled him. His threat didn't bother me—I still had my Police Special in my jacket, and even without it I suspected I could take the older, slower man without serious trouble—but I didn't need to spend any time in the local jail. What was making Grinder so edgy? Either he didn't want me talking to Darryl, or else he was more cunning than I thought and had found this way of sending me on the wrong trail.

I saw a mailbox ahead with the number that the phone book had given as Darryl's address. It was at the end of a drive leading thirty feet back to a little saltbox house, wearing shabby gray siding. The snowy yard held a crisscross of tire marks, and in the backyard I could glimpse a jungle gym rusting to oblivion.

The house looked dark, and no car stood in the driveway. No one answered my knock, so I tested the door and found it locked. Evergreen shrubs hid the house from the neighbors. I walked around the place, looking for an open window. They were all secure, and the back door was locked as well. I didn't have a pick set with me, and I needed to learn more before breaking and entering.

Not far from the dilapidated jungle gym I saw a black smear against the lingering snow. It looked like the remnants of a bonfire, a pile of gray ash and the charcoal fossils of burned trunks. A pile of pine trimmings, needles brown and desiccated, lay near the ashes. Pine saplings, I saw, all cut in three- or four-foot sections, the largest an inch in diameter at the base.

Oddly for such small trees, the sticks were branchless, except for a couple that sprouted a few sprays near the very top. If I assembled the top and bottom section, I had an eight-foot tall, nearly branchless pine tree, something Charlie Brown might see in nightmares at Christmas time.

Something else odd: each tree had been marked with a splotch of blue spray paint. I broke off a sprig from one of the trees with brown needles, seeming as fragile as three-thousand-year-old papyrus, walked back to the Jeep, and set it in the back seat.

The sun had gone down. I drove a little further on High Street, getting a sense of the ridgeline area. The road twisted like a snake, making it hard to see more than a hundred feet ahead. The houses got further apart, except one stretch where three houses clustered together, parts and chunks of about twenty junked cars sharing their collective yard.

I turned around there, but before I could pull back into the street my cell phone rang. I expected Gina, but I heard Jerry Smith's voice: "Tyler?"

"Yeah."

"Listen, I'm sorry. I blew it there in the diner. Look, I've been under strain, you know? That's not an excuse, but, well, for what it's worth, I apologize."

"Thanks, kid. Say, while I've got you on the phone, where did Jeremiah live?"

"In a trailer park north of Northfield."

"What's the name?"

"What does it matter?"

I didn't press it; Jeremiah had told me about the trailer park, but I hadn't noticed it when I drove up Route 12. "Jerry, why did you pretend you didn't know Eva Benson?"

I heard his breathing. I suspected he was mentally replaying our conversation. "Did I say I didn't know her? We went to the same high school, that's all. I didn't really know her."

"But you must have recognized her when Jeremiah took you to Benson's place."

He grunted. "Oakley, I called to apologize. But I'm serious about firing you. If you want to do something for Jeremiah, honor his grandson's request."

"Don't you want to know who killed him? Or who tied you to that tree, and why?"

"The police will find the hit-and-run driver. My business is my business."

"Jerry, it wasn't a hit-and-run accident. It was deliberate murder." I wondered what would happen if I stirred the pot. "I have an eyewitness."

"Who?"

"I could only give that information to my employer."

"I could tell the police you're hiding information."

"You could. But it wouldn't solve anything. It wouldn't help you find out who killed your grandfather."

"Look, just drop it."

"Then tell me about Bill Grinder."

"It's late, and we're on a tight deadline. Sorry." He hung up.

I turned off the phone. I dislike phones, dislike e-mail and instant messaging and all the other forms of communication that seem to be replacing face-to-face discussion. You can't see the other person's expressions or body language. You can't judge when they begin to lie. You can't punch them in the nose.

I pulled out into High Street and drove back toward town, and not long after I had passed Darryl's driveway a red Dodge muscle truck swung around the curve ahead. My headlights were on, and thanks to them and the dying light of sunset, I recognized Darryl at the wheel. The truck bed had been loaded high with pine saplings. After he had vanished behind me, I made a U-turn and drove back to his house. The truck was in the drive and lights were on in the house. I checked the safety on my Police Special, but left it in my jacket pocket.

Darryl opened the door before I could knock. "What do you want?"

I pushed forward, bumping his shoulder as he made a half-hearted attempt to block me. "We need to talk."

He hadn't shaved in a day or two. From close up I could see the ghost of a blond beard on his chin and upper lip. His skin was sallow and blue veins showed through it. He wore faded blue jeans, a gray-green flannel shirt, and brown lace-up work boots. I smelled stale beer, pizza, cigarettes, and the faint reek of pot.

"I'm not talking to you except to tell you to leave. You ain't welcome, Tyler."

We were in a poor man's living room, dark wood paneled walls, a ceiling painted yellow but peeling here and there, a brown shag rug at least twenty years old and matted with spills. The couch and recliner were shabby, the pine coffee table scarred and cigarette-burned. But against the far wall a brand new big-screen TV stood on an improvised entertainment center made from scavenged milk crates.

Beside the jam-packed ashtray on the pine table lay a corncob pipe. I picked it up and sniffed it. "Smoking a little dope, Darryl?"

He convulsively grabbed for the pipe, and I let him take it from my hand. "None of your damn business!" He started to drop the pipe into his pocket, hesitated, and then turned and tossed it into the fireplace. A fire had been laid out but not lit. "Get out of here," he said. "Or I'll call the police."

"Call them. I'd like to talk to them."

He lowered his chin and glowered at me. I didn't think he'd start a fistfight that he knew he'd lose. He was younger and taller than me, but in sloppy shape, with a little bulge of belly and slack muscles. Maybe hoping to needle him into trying me on, I said, "Are you this way with all Wanda's friends?"

His face turned red. "I've got a shotgun in my bedroom!"

"And I've got a thirty-eight Police Special even closer. Want to play cops and robbers?"

He looked uncertainly at my hand stuck down into my jacket pocket. "Like hell you've got a gun."

So I pulled the revolver out and casually aimed it at the center of his new TV. "I could show you how it works."

"Put it away," he said.

I sat down in the recliner with the gun in my lap. "Just remember I can use it quicker than you can get to your shotgun. What did you do with your hunting rifle, Darryl?"

His face took on an assumed expression of stupidity. "I don't know what you mean."

"How long have you had that TV? High def, is it? I hear they're pretty expensive."

"I had it a while. Look, I got stuff to do. OK, you got the gun, you're the man. You made the point. Leave, OK?"

"Nice boots. What size are they?"

"Huh? Nines."

"Did you take a shot at Jeremiah and me on my land a couple of days ago?"

"What? No! Get out of my—"

"Shut up. If you and Bill Grinder are up to something illegal, more illegal than smoking dope, say, if you've been doing something for Caleb Benson and being paid in cash, you really haven't left yourself many options. Between the police asking you and me asking you, which would you prefer?"

He was a chameleon, this Darryl boy. Now his neck and ears reddened. "I won't answer no questions. If you try me on, I'll beat the living shit out of you. I'm telling you, get the hell out of my house."

"Why are you burning the pine saplings out back?"

He opened the door and said, "Get the hell out!"

I walked past him and paused a step in front of him. "Ever been hit by a stun gun, Darryl?" I poked him in the stomach with two fingers, and he thrashed like a gaffed salmon.

I drove back through Northfield. The early night had come on clear and colder. I headed up Route 12 to the EZ Living Mobile Home Park and pulled in. Four streets forked off from the main entrance, and alongside them huddled mobile homes ranging from rusted and elderly models to fancy new almost-a-house ones. They had practically no yards, but the place seemed to have been kept up well enough. I got out of my Jeep beside a rack of mailboxes and used my halogen flashlight to find one marked J. Smith. It was for trailer 2-23.

Figuring that 2 was the street, I took the second street from the left. Odd numbers were on the right, and halfway down the street I found Jeremiah's place. The mobile home wasn't new, and I guessed it was a two-bedroom one, judging from length and the arrangement of windows. It was a faded blue, and Smith, or someone, had built a wooden porch that ran half the length of the trailer. It also had a steeply pitched roof built on peeling, weathered two-by-four pillars that kept the heavy Vermont snow from accumulating on a flat roof.

Nobody was about. I parked and went up on the porch as if confidently expecting Jeremiah would be home. My flashlight showed a wood plaque mounted on the trailer just to the right of the door. It looked as if a kid had made it with a wood-burning set: WELCOME TO THE RESIDENCE OF JEREMIAH SMITH.

The storm door and front door were both unlocked, saving me the bother of forcing them or going back to my cabin for a lock pick set. I stepped inside Smith's living room and my flashlight beam showed me I wasn't the first to visit. Someone had tossed aside the cushions from the sofa and recliner. All the cabinets in the kitchen stood open, pots and pans and canned goods lay where they had fallen, and even the trash bin had been upended.

I closed the curtains and turned on the lights, then walked down the hall. The first bedroom was fixed up as an office, with a desk, an old Underwood Standard portable typewriter, and a wall full of thumbtacked photos and mementoes of his years with the city. I pulled the drapes closed and turned on the lights. On a four-by-six foot corkboard hung black and white and faded color pictures of a younger Jeremiah Smith. One showed him and several other men around a huge snow-plow. Yellowed newspaper clippings commemorated record blizzards. Newer articles about forestry, logging, and the passage or repeal of various laws overhung the older stuff.

Here, too, the place had been ransacked. The desk drawers hung open, one actually standing on end on the floor. A tumble of rolled-up white-and-blue survey charts and topographic maps had fallen out of the open closet door.

The bathroom next door had been searched. At the far end of the hall, the bedroom had suffered, too: the mattress of an unmade bed lay half-on, half-off the box springs and the dresser drawers and closet had been plundered. Whoever had made the search hadn't been looking for something small or easily concealed: the cushions had not been slashed, the coffee and flour packages hadn't been dumped. None of the framed pictures, mostly of Vermont wildlife, had been taken from the walls. Whatever the searcher had looked for was small enough to fit in the cabinet beneath the bathroom sink, but too large to hide behind a picture or in a box of cereal.

I gravitated back to Smith's office. The old metal desk with a gray rubberized surface probably dated from the 1950s— town surplus, I guessed—and the top was clear except for the typewriter and three shriveled things that turned out to be dried mushrooms, one black, one brown with small white and pink spots, and a long, thin one that was the pale gray color of a body three hours dead. They seemed in pristine condition. I didn't pick them up but stooped to examine them closely. What had they meant to Jeremiah? Edibles he'd picked in the forest? Somebody's gift to him? Rare specimens? In the living room, I had noticed a shelf that held a collection of old bottles, some with faded labels still on them, all neatly arranged so they could be seen. It appeared Smith was interested in mushrooms.

In the open desk drawer on the left I found a stack of typing paper. There was also an organizer with pencils, pens, rubber bands, and paper clips in separate compartments. Jeremiah had been a man who took care of his things, gave each one its place. In the old photos the men around Jeremiah stood close to him, threw an arm over his shoulder. I got the sense of a decent and caring human being, one who knew things most people didn't, one who loved the long history of the area and his knowledge of the secrets of the forest, of the Abenaki.

But something hit me. None of the photos showed Jerry, none showed Jeremiah's deceased daughter or wife. I held my flashlight close to the walls and scanned them with a flattened beam. On the wall were five nails with small heads, one centered right over the desk. A faint tracing of dust showed me where five eight-by-ten frames had once hung. I wondered if Jerry had come to get the family photos. I didn't think Jeremiah would have taken them down. I had the feeling that he would have treasured the reminders of his family, particularly of Rebecca, the wife he'd spoken of with an obvious, lingering love.

I checked the large desk drawer underneath the one that held supplies. Hanging folders were in perfect order, a series of tabs slanting left to right in a diagonal line. The front folders had been labeled with years, starting in 1981. Tax records, I guessed after a look at one folder. Behind them were alphabetically-arranged folders: ABENAKI, and behind that BILLS, CORRESPONDENCE, FORESTS, JERRY, NATURAL RESOURCES AGENCY, REBECCA, SUSAN.

The JERRY file was full of letters, report cards, medical records, and the general detritus of life, as were REBECCA and SUSAN. NATURAL RESOURCES held brochures about hunting seasons and regulations, a guide to wild animal tracks, a half-inch-thick government publication summarizing the state laws concerning the use of resources in Vermont. The FORESTS file included a clipping of Jerry's article about gene-jumping, and another of his story on genetically modified foods, plus roughly thirty pages of what looked like taxation boundaries superimposed on topographic maps. In the lower right corner of each was the word TRACT followed by a hyphenated number. I put that file on top of the desk.

Jeremiah's CORRESPONDENCE file went back a little more than ten years. At random I pulled out faded carbon copies of letters Jeremiah had sent to state and local politicians. He advocated the passage of laws to protect Vermont's wilderness areas. He argued that hunters should be restricted to preserves—that areas where hunting was legal should have been posted, not areas where it was prohibited.

I pulled out one carbon that had been stapled to a reply. It was a couple of years old. The address was in Massachusetts.

I read Jeremiah's letter first:

Dear Genotypes Consolidated,

My old friend Caleb Benson often speaks highly of your products and services, and I may be doing some work similar to his research. Could you please send me a copy of your most recent catalog? Also, could you confirm that Caleb is your customer—I may have mixed up the companies in my addled old head, and don't want to embarrass myself by telling him I can't remember which company he'd so highly recommended when he's probably mentioned them (I think it's you) a dozen times over the past year or two.

Sincerely,
Jeremiah Smith, PhD
Research Forester

The company's response letter had been done on a laser printer. Beneath a well-designed logo that incorporated a microscope and an Erlenmeyer flask, the response said:

Dear Dr. Smith,

Thank you for your interest in our products. As you can see from the enclosed catalog, they are among the most advanced for their price in the industry. We've outfitted hundreds of small labs around the world, and some have made significant breakthroughs in their particular areas of research. We help them keep their budget focused on research and personnel by supplying basic equipment at a reasonable price, and offering a comprehensive leasing program for more specialized equipment such as our SQ-10L Spectrographic Sequence Analyzer.

Please pass along our thanks to Mr. Benson for his recommendation. As I'm sure he's told you, his associate Frank Lauser has been a regular customer of ours for years, so no doubt we are the company he referenced. I'll thank him for the referral the next time I hear from him as well.

If I can be of any service to you, our toll-free number is above and my extension is 3134.

It was signed by Deborah S. Colledge, Associate Director of Marketing, Scientific and Laboratory Products. I looked back in the file and found the catalog she had sent. I could recognize beakers, test tubes, and Petri dishes, but I could only imagine what their comprehensive list of special products and services was about—transcription in vitro, mutagenesis, DNA sequencing, gene screening and purification, and something that sounded comically ominous: mouse knockouts.

Nothing else in the CORRESPONDENCE file seemed meaningful, but I stacked the catalog atop the FORESTS file. BILLS was empty, but the ABENAKI file was fat with years of newspaper clippings, flyers and donation receipts from the Dawnland Center in Montpelier, and a batch of historical and contemporary literature from the Abenaki tribal headquarters up north. I added it to the pile.

Then somebody banged on the trailer's door. I didn't realize how edgy I had been until I found myself flubbing a quick draw from my jacket pocket. I grabbed the files from the desk and switched off the lights as I headed toward the door. I put the gun back in my pocket and began to run my story through my head. To my immense relief, the person standing on Jeremiah's porch wasn't a lawman. It was a little old lady, hands cupped around her eyes as she peered in through the storm door.

But then, I've known little old ladies who were harder to face down than a cop.

18

took a second, and the woman and I just looked at each other. I made no effort to hide the files I held, or to reach for my weapon. I was in my client's home, doing work for him. I opened the storm door to a woman in her seventies, graying hair pulled back in a severe bun. She looked upset, and when I stepped onto the porch she took three quick steps back. "Can I help you?" I asked.

"Who are you?"

"My name is Oakley Tyler. I'm a friend of Jeremiah's."

"Somebody really tore up his place," she said, staring past me at the couch cushions.

"Not me. Have you seen anybody over here in the last couple of days besides me and Jerry?"

She frowned, pulling her gray eyebrows together. She had the look of a nineteenth-century schoolmarm. I could picture her marching between rows of desks with a ruler ready to slap knuckles. "I knew I should have called the police," she muttered.

"Tell me about it. I'm working with the police," I said, stretching a point to the limit of its capacity.

"A man came by this morning. I didn't recognize him. Young man."

"He must have been the one who made the mess, then, Miss—"

"Mrs. Frieda Schmidt," she said, and spelled it. "I live next door. I saw the lights on over here. What are you doing?"

I showed her the files and improvised. "I came to pick up some work that Jeremiah was pulling together for me. He told me I could drop by anytime. He said if he wasn't here I could just go in and pick up these files. He told me where they'd be."

"But he's dead."

"He told me earlier this week, when he visited my house. He hired me to look into something for him. I'm a private investigator."

"Oh."

"Actually, I was just leaving." I reached in and turned off the porch light, then pulled the door shut behind me. "Should I lock this?" I asked. "I can set the lock if you think I should, but I don't know if Jerry has a key."

She shook her head. "Jeremiah never locked it. He might not even have had the key any longer. To me, that's asking for trouble. I've had a security system installed myself. We're only four hours from Boston, and you know the kind of people who live there. Murders every day, home invasions, I don't know."

I saw that two other neighbors stood silhouetted in their windows, watching us in the glow of the streetlight. It made me itch to get out of there, but I said, "Tell me about the young man you saw this morning."

She bobbed her head like a pigeon. "It was early, eight-thirty. I was still in my bathrobe. I heard him stop his car and looked out my window and saw him as he went in." She looked thoughtful. "He was tall, a little taller than you. Blond with an average kind of haircut. I couldn't see him well enough for much detail. I'm nearsighted, and the window was frosted over."

"Did you see what he was driving?"

"Oh, yes, a red pickup truck."

I nodded. "I know who that is. He lives in Northfield, but he wouldn't have had permission from Jeremiah or Jerry. Could you tell if he took anything from the trailer?"

"He did! It was a plastic trash bag. Not the biggest kind, more like a kitchen bag." She furrowed her brow. "He carried it in the middle, as if there was a lamp or something like that in it. Or—" she glanced at the trailer door—"could it have been a gun?"

"Was it long enough to be a rifle?"

"No. But it might have been like, what do they call it, like an Uzi. It was long enough for that." She stepped closer and confided, "But I don't think it was. Jeremiah never owned a gun that I knew of. Do you think I should have called the police, Mr. Tyler?"

"I can't say. If he comes again, I'd advise you to call 911. If he goes back inside, tell them it's a burglary in progress."

"That young man shouldn't have made such a mess. It's not respectful. Jeremiah's dead."

"You didn't tell me—have you noticed Jerry coming to the trailer?"

"I haven't, but I'm not home all the time, I'm often over at Margaret's house during the days, which is a full street over. I know Jerry by sight. Never talked to him much. Jeremiah was sociable enough, but Jerry never had much time for neighbors when he lived here."

"Oh, he stayed with Jeremiah?"

"A couple of times, a year or two ago. Just briefly, like visits."

"Did he have anyone with him? A girlfriend, any other friends?"

"No, just Jerry."

I thanked Mrs. Schmidt and walked her to the street with good-byes, put the files on the floor under the passenger seat, and drove back toward town.

◆

On impulse, I drove out High Street, and slowed down as I passed Darryl's house. In the backyard the pile of little trees blazed red-orange.

Now why was Darryl burning saplings? I decided to ask him. I backed in next to his truck and walked around to the fire. He was leaning against the house, and he held the hunting rifle he'd had this morning. I'd made no effort to be quiet, and he looked at me, his face invisible in the darkness. I knew the fire illuminated me, and I saw him swing the rifle barrel up.

"I told you to get off my property!" His voice held a little more authority, borrowed from his rifle. "I meant to stay off it, too."

The Police Special was in my right hand. My left, in the pocket, held my cell phone. I raised my revolver so it pointed at his legs, as his rifle aimed at mine. "You going to shoot me, Darryl?"

"Man's got a right to shoot trespassers!"

"So I could have plugged you on my land this morning, nice and legally? What are you burning, Darryl?"

"Scrap wood," he said quickly. "Too green for the fireplace or the woodstove."

"Pretty small, too. Why not just let it rot?"

"I don't have to answer any questions!" He jerked the rifle up with a suddenness I had not expected. It weaved in a small circle, but it was pointed toward my chest. "I could shoot you on the spot."

I realized that he had not even registered that I held the pistol. I raised it and said, "Me, too. Self-defense, unprovoked attack during a perfectly civil visit. I don't see any No Tres-passing signs posted. You haven't registered your property, Darryl."

"Shit!" The barrel of his rifle was weaving wildly, as if he found the weapon too heavy. "If you shot me on my own property, they'd throw you so deep in prison you'd never see daylight again."

One step sideways took me out of the firelight. "Darryl, I don't think you'd shoot me. I don't think you'd want the police involved." I swept my revolver to the side and shot out one of his truck headlights.

Darryl jerked. "Jesus! Why the hell didja do that?"

"Let's call the police, Darryl. I've done something illegal, firing a weapon so close to your house, damaging your property. I've got my cell phone. Let's call the police and you can tell them about it."

He walked to the side, sighted carefully, and shot out the passenger-side taillight of my Jeep. "You want to go on? You want me to shoot you right now?"

"I'll leave if you'll tell me what you took out of Jeremiah Smith's trailer. That's burglary, Darryl. Two to five on a first conviction."

"You shot first," Darryl said, as if trying to talk himself into something. "Whatever I do, it's self-defense."

"Do you need to pee?" I asked.

"Huh?"

"I bet I can pee farther than you can."

To my surprise, Darryl giggled. "I get it. We're acting like fifth graders." He lowered the barrel of his rifle. "Shit." He shook his head. "Look, just go. I don't think we're even, but that's OK. I ain't gonna talk to you, and you ain't gonna call the cops. Just go."

"OK, Darryl." I got into the Jeep, cursing myself. John Lincoln would be laughing himself silly somewhere. You never get into dumb-ass macho games, never. As I turned toward town I heard the bang of the rifle and the crash as my driver's side taillight shattered. Darryl was a better shot than I'd sized him up to be.

I was hungry. The CLT had worn off, so I stopped at the market and picked up salad fixings and a fresh loaf of bread. I kind of hoped Sylvia would be waiting for me, and I thought she might like this kind of fare.

I drove up the logging road to within sight of my cabin, farther than I normally do because it's so much trouble to back down the narrow, rutted path. Kerosene lantern light shone in the windows. I retrieved the files under the seat and swung out with them and the bag of food, eager to see Sylvia again. As I set foot on the porch, I fleetingly wondered what I would do if it were Bill Grinder inside.

But I saw Sylvia look out the window. I felt a wave of relief. She was nutty, by my standards—maybe by common standards—but she had the kind of integrity you don't find in tobacco execs who brag that they are responsibly marketing their products in the United States, not bothering to mention that at the same time they're busily addicting preteens in developing nations.

Sylvia opened the door for me and glanced at the files in my hands and the grocery bag clutched in the crook of my elbows. She took the bag from me lightly, tentatively, and I tossed the files onto my bed.

"How are you?" I asked. "Hungry?"

"I ate with my people," she said. She set the bag down on the counter. "Should I leave while you eat?"

"No. Are your people nearby now?"

She inclined her head, not quite a negative gesture, but it told me she wasn't interested in talking about her people at the moment. I sat in the bentwood rocker and she took the straight one, as always. "I really don't know anything about you," I said. "Are you married? Do you have children?"

"I'm not married," she said. "I have two offspring."

"How old?"

She looked as if she were wrestling with the concept of age. "Mature," she said at last.

"They don't have a father?"

"Oh, they have a father." She smiled. "He is the father of others, as well. But let us speak of something else."

I sighed. "Maybe you can tell me about the Abenaki. I'm thinking that Jeremiah's death could somehow be tied to his defense of the tribe."

Sylvia stared at the floor. "The Abenaki were good members of the family of life, a long time ago, before Europeans came." She looked almost as if she were drifting into a trance. "They could teach your people much. They suffered greatly under the French and the British. Then the Americans hunted them because some of them had allied with the French. Not many are left, but they have wisdom. They would not endanger all life as you do."

"Me?"

"I mean your people. You are of your people's spirit. You carry that spirit. I don't mean you as an individual. You are not like so many of them."

"That's because I'm a mongrel," I told her. "My mother's grandfather bought his wife—my great-grandmother—as a slave and then took her as his wife. She was part Irish and part Indian, though she was taken very young and no one knows what tribe she was from. On the other side, my grandfather's family came from Northern Europe in the late nineteenth century. They were from Scandinavia—explorers and pirates. None of them fit in very well with proper European society."

"It is not just blood," she said softly. "I sense a deep sadness in you. You have known great loss, and you have spent much of your life in the gray shadows, where there are no clear boundaries between right and wrong. You have empathy for others, a rare quality among whites. You share that with the Abenaki. I doubt you could hear their story without weeping."

"Maybe. But I've read that some Native Americans weren't the good stewards of the land they're portrayed as being. Some tribes slaughtered buffalo just for their tongues, burned forests to drive out game, destroyed rather than refrained from interfering."

"That is true and it is not," she said. "You must understand that cultures have their own lives, their own cycles. Not just humans, but all forms of life. It is true some tribes were wasteful and thoughtless, but in their cycle things were different. When there are many, many rabbits, the foxes have larger litters. More foxes the next year means fewer rabbits, and the year after, foxes grow thin and their litters become smaller. Eventually they reach a balance."

"So the wasteful Native Americans were really just part of a cycle."

She looked at me then, a speculative expression in her brown eyes. "Ten thousand years ago, when the mountains of blue ice were melting northward, the ancestors of the Abenaki first came here. Then food was abundant, and they killed wantonly, as their people had for centuries while they crossed the continent. They and others hunted whole species to extinction: the giant ground sloth, the glyptodont, the woolly mammoth. Animals here were easy prey, for they had not learned to fear man. And so the early people flourished, had large families, and believed they were in paradise."

"But they reached a limit?"

She rocked gently and nodded. "They overfished and overhunted. They fought each other for food during a time when winters were harsh and summers short; they killed each other. It was a time of great violence, some thousands of years ago. They had learned a bitter lesson that others all over the world have learned, to their cost: when the balance was tipped, there would not be enough for all, so they fought over what was left. Those who stole or saved the most food gained power during the times of hunger."

"Something similar happened in Europe during a climate shift we call the Little Ice Age," I said.

"It has happened many places, many times. All growth takes its own pace. And this was a time of great misery, when a few had much and most had little. Violence and hunger ruled. Yes, the people awakened, but slowly. Generations passed before the last of the . . . cannibals? Before the last cannibals were seen as so insane that the people no longer allowed them to seize power."

"Cannibals?"

"*Wétiko*," she said, emphasizing the first syllable. "It means those who live by taking life from others. It is what many native people called whites many years later. No, they don't literally eat other people, but they take slaves, they take the fruit of others' work, and so in a sense they eat the lives of others."

"And then what happened?"

"Those who were to become the Abenaki learned from Grandmother Groundhog, who taught Gluscabe and rejoined the cycle, the one that always comes when rabbits are many and foxes few, and then reverses. Your people need to understand this. They need to know that eating the life of Earth is like cannibalism. You used coal for a long time, and now you use oil and gas as well. It poisons the world, and yet every year you consume more and more of it. If you do not wake up from your dream, when the world is poisoned and things begin to die, then the time of terror, the violence, begins, on a larger scale than ever before."

She looked very sad. "It is here, the time of killing," she added softly. "Since I last saw you, millions of lives have been taken by humans. Twenty thousand have died of starvation. The terror has already begun."

"Can we end it?"

"If you awaken. If not, the time of terror is very near for America, for China, for many other greedy nations. You are like the fat men who hoarded the food in the time of the Abenaki troubles. You must awaken, or you will suffer with the rest of the world."

I said, "Yes, but if we could master fusion or learn how to efficiently harness solar power—"

She got up, went to the stove, opened it, and put in some wood. I felt a yearning for her, not a desire for casual sex, but the primal need to know this woman completely, in every sense of the word. She returned to the chair and said, "Did you see what I did?"

"You put wood in the stove."

She shook her head. "I have set the sun free."

"Oh. The wood captured sunlight through photosynthesis and stored the energy, and when you burn the wood, the energy of the sun is released again."

"The sunlight that now comes from your stove fell to Earth during the time of your father, or maybe even within your own life. But the sunlight that runs your car fell to Earth millions of years ago. You cannot speed that process. When the oil is gone, it is gone—for the next four hundred million years, at least. You are like foxes during a time of many rabbits now, but the abundance will end. Your people's arrogance destroys too much life, threatens the world, threatens your people and mine."

"Why tell me this?"

"Because you are not afraid to interfere."

"You said interference was wrong."

"And killing is wrong. But sometimes killing is necessary." She looked miserable. "This is what you do. This is who you are. You move in shadow, where the boundaries are faint. It takes a man or woman like you." She was silent for so long that I got up from my chair and began to make my dinner.

She watched as I built the salad in my big yard-sale mixing bowl, watched as I drizzled olive oil over the greens and tossed them. "Are you sure you won't have some?" I asked. I brought the bowl over. She tilted her head, looking at the salad. She reached tentatively, plucked out a leaf of romaine lettuce, and shook the oil from it. She took a nibble, then greedily pulled the whole leaf into her mouth and chewed.

Impulsively, I knelt beside her, picked out another piece of lettuce, and held it to her mouth. She took it from my fingers with her lips. I found the ritual oddly touching, and I hand fed her until she had finished the bowl. My own hunger seemed to have dissipated. I put the empty bowl in the sink and wiped my hands with a towel, then gently patted her lips with it.

"You are extraordinary," I said. I traced the line of her lips with my forefinger, and she very tentatively touched my skin with her tongue. I cupped her face between my hands and kissed her forehead. She smelled of forest and leather and tasted faintly salty. She turned her head, took my little finger into her mouth, and sucked on it. That aroused me instantly.

Then she pulled away, releasing my finger, eyes wide and nostrils flared.

I backed off. "I'm sorry. I didn't mean to frighten you."

She lowered her head and I heard her sniffle. "You and I are too different. We cannot be close. There are stories of how your people and mine sometimes mated. They are tragic."

"But one of my ancestors was a Native American."

"You don't understand. I belong there." She waved toward the door, indicating, I supposed, the forest.

"Isn't it dangerous out there?" I asked.

"Grandfather is nearby to protect me." She saw my puzzled look and said, "The Grandfather of the forest. You call him bear."

"But bears hibernate," I said.

"These are grave times. The weather has changed. The world is dying. Grandfather and others protect me, so I can speak to you." She clasped her hands in her lap. "I have to awaken you. You must know, must understand that the myths of your people are myths, no matter how well-intentioned. You must know that all the easy stories are wrong. The truth is larger and more encompassing. You must learn the wisdom of Earth, that all living things must live in harmony, that when some are tempted by abundance then disharmony and death result." She glanced over at my bed, where the files lay. "Above all, you must know that writing words down is not capturing wisdom. You may record knowledge, and others may profit from it, but wisdom comes not from words, but from life. And the clever, the manipulative, mistake knowledge for power." She said, "Jeremiah Smith knew this. It led to his dying."

"How?"

A sob escaped from her. "Don't you feel how important it is not to interfere?"

"But you just said I had to, that you were sent to ask me to interfere."

"Yes. And I hate myself for it. I am asking you to do that which I fear to do myself."

"What do you mean?"

She looked away and in a miserable voice said, "If a person went to the place where a man was tied to a tree, went early in the morning, and stood against that tree and faced the sun . . . if he raised his right arm straight by his side, pointing straight to his right, and then walked in that direction, he would find . . . something."

"Walked? How far?"

"Until he found it. He would know."

"What will I find?"

She stood up. "I must leave."

I got out of my chair and stood facing her. I reached out and put my hand on her arm. She was trembling. "Sylvia—" I began, and then my cell phone rang.

She jumped back two feet, knocking the chair into the woodstove. It fell sideways with a clatter. She righted the chair as I answered the phone.

"Tell me you didn't shoot up Darryl's car," said the voice. It was Wanda.

"Let me call you back," I said.

"What, you picked up another waitress?"

Sylvia had backed away and stood giving me a head-tilted look. I conveyed my apology with my eyes, and she looked down at the rug, but she stayed where she was. I said into the phone, "Wanda, I'm sorry. I was an asshole. I should have stayed in touch."

"Yeah, like I'd want you to." But her sarcasm lacked sting. "Look, Gina Berkof called me this evening and wanted to know what was up with you. And I heard from the wife of the guy who lives right across from Darryl's place that Darryl and somebody with a Jeep were firing off shots at each other's cars."

"He started it."

Wanda gave me a mama-snort. "Darryl's in trouble," she said. "And I think you are, too, Oakley. What's this about?"

"It's about some trees he was burning in back of his house."

"I don't believe you. That's supposed to make sense?"

"What makes you say he's in trouble?"

She took her time before answering: "I thought I loved Darryl at one time. He's really a decent person, deep down inside. He's got that whole dumb act that got him through his childhood, but he's really pretty smart. Lately he's changed, though—he's secretive, he's throwing around money that he shouldn't have, and he's tangling with you." She paused again and then said, "Is it true that you used to be in the CIA?"

"Where'd you hear that?"

"Bernie at the bookstore. He's reading some book about your old partner. Says that Lincoln started a private practice with an ex-CIA agent."

"That was all a lifetime ago. I'm long since retired."

"Spies don't retire."

I felt a weary kind of embarrassment. Everybody knows what spies are like—blend together bad TV shows, James Bond movies, and sex fantasies and you have a spy. That's not the truth. "I'm not a spy or a private eye now, Wanda," I said.

"Then Darryl's not working for you, for the government?"

"He's not doing anything for or with me."

"Then why did you go to see him?"

"To ask what he was doing on my property this morning. He and Bill Grinder showed up with rifles."

"They must have been rabbit hunting."

"So they said. What did Gina Berkof ask you?"

"She's single, you know."

"Wanda, I—"

I heard her sigh. "Sorry. That was a cheap shot. We're over, Oakley, that's all. I have a daughter who I love. The last thing I need is some half-crazy spy raising hell and shooting at people."

"It won't happen again, and I'm happy if we can just be friends. What did Gina say?"

"She told me to ask you to call her at home. She has news about a car. You need her number?"

"Shoot."

She rattled off the number, and I wrote it down. Then Wanda said, "Look, leave Darryl alone, OK? There's no harm in him. Whatever you're up to, keep him out of it." She hung up.

I looked over at Sylvia, still planted in the same spot. "I need to make a call. Will you wait?"

She did not respond, and I took that for silent assent. Gina Berkof answered on the third ring. I identified myself, and she said, "Sorry it took me so long to get back to you. I lost your number, so I called Wanda. Anyhow, I got a look at the police logs. I checked with Northfield and Montpelier, and neither had anything, but there was a dark blue Subaru wagon stopped by state cops on Route Eighty-Nine, heading into Burlington. They stopped to check for drunk driving, but the guy tested sober, so they checked his license and let him go."

"Who owned the car?"

"Discount Rentals at the Burlington Airport.

"And the driver's name?"

"Frank Lauser." I stiffened.

"I called the rental car company, too," Gina said. "I told them Lauser had left some papers in a booth at a restaurant, and I had picked them up and wanted to return them. Looked like a deed, I told them. They were nice as anything, gave me his address. Ready?"

"Go ahead."

"Address is listed as PO Box 72434, Newark, New Jersey, and the girl couldn't make out the Zip. Is this the guy who creamed Jerry's grandpa?"

"No, I don't think so. Did you happen to get the car's plate number?"

"I didn't. Should have written it down. I do remember they were Vermont plates, registered to the car agency, but that's all."

"Thanks, Gina," I said. "That's a big help."

"I actually sort of enjoyed it," she said with a laugh. "Made me feel like a real reporter again instead of a space-filler for a poky little weekly. You know, when I was straight out of college I worked for the *Boston Globe*."

"What happened?"

"I did a story on a major corporation that wasn't exactly flattering. The editor didn't want to run it because I couldn't get an inside source, making her wary of a lawsuit. So I fired myself before they quit me."

"I didn't know you were an activist."

She laughed again. "I wouldn't call myself that. I'm a rationalist. OK, so the Supreme Court says a corporation is a person. So I say when a corporation is guilty of a capital crime, it should get the death penalty."

"Lethal injection?"

"No, but states can pull the charters of corporations. It never happens, though. States can execute individuals, but individuals can't put politicians in office, and corporations can—one hand washes the other. Hope I've helped, Tyler. See you around."

I hung up and walked over to Sylvia. I took her hands in mine, surprised at how rough and strong they felt. I slipped my arms around her waist and drew her to me. She stood rigid for a moment, and I felt her breasts flatten against my chest. She sighed and leaned into me, her temple against my cheek. Then she put her arms around me and pulled me tight against her, as though she were trying to melt into me, and I felt her hands stroking my back.

I tried to kiss her, but she turned her head away. "Sorry," I muttered, feeling clumsy and brutish.

She caught my right earlobe in her teeth and tugged it, and I moved to hold her closer.

But Sylvia trembled, then slowed her breath and relaxed, still holding me, still moving against me. Her hand moved around my thigh, to my hip, to the small of my back.

"Stay with me," I said huskily. "Spend the night."

But then she withdrew, pushed away from me, ran to the door, threw it open, and bolted into the night.

19

I walked to the open door. The night air felt like a wall between two worlds. The moon lit the forest with a faint glow, but I could see no detail in a landscape painted with gray and the eggshell-white of moonlight. Nothing stirred—not Sylvia, not Grandfather Bear.

I thought again of Wanda and the night we'd spent together, all the laughs and touches, the sidelong glances, the way we'd talked through our terrible bowling games. It had been a dance of life, with perhaps each of us using the other, the way people do, a night of sweetness and release. Once we had been to bed, the geography of our lives shifted subtly, took away our pretended innocence, our excuse for playing. We could either make it something serious after that, or we could let it sour and darken into pretend fun, curdled love.

Something swooped overhead in a jerky flight pattern: the thaw had woken one hibernating bat. He'd be a hungry bat if he didn't head south. No insects were available for him this early in the year. I heard the gurgle of water and realized the snow melt was going on beneath the crusted surface. The cold snap had passed and the night was nearly balmy. How would

I have felt if Sylvia had accepted my invitation to spend the night? What games would the two of us have played?

Then something large moved down the slope to the right, at the edge of the forest, lumbering away fast in a loping stride. I couldn't make out any detail, but it wasn't human. I called, "Good night, Grandfather," and closed the door.

I poured a glass of red wine and picked up my cell phone. Laid down on the bed with a spiral-bound pad and a pen at the ready, propped myself up on two pillows, and called 411. I asked for the number of Frank Lauser, Newark, New Jersey. No such listing. None for any F. Lausers. They did have Lauser's Electronic Repair, a Michael Lauser, and a Teresa Lauser, but that was it. No Frank Lauser in the whole area code, for that matter.

I drank half my wine quickly, enjoying the taste, the spreading warmth. There had been times, not many, when John Lincoln and I got stinking drunk. It was bad for him, and he knew it. He was the kind of alcoholic who could stay sober for eleven months, then go on a week-long bender. The drink had killed him, along with painkillers and stimulants, the things he used to mask the damage his profession had done to his body and soul, to rouse himself to extra effort. I set my half-empty glass on the floor, wondering if I'd burned out completely.

I hadn't worked since John died, but my efforts on behalf of Jeremiah Smith reminded me how much I'd loved the game, being the hunter, occasionally the hunted. But I was spinning my wheels. Who had shot at us? Who'd stuck a flare into Jeremiah's truck? Who'd driven the car that had smacked him into eternity, who had tied Jerry to the tree, and why had it all been done?

I favored Bill Grinder as a suspect, but I couldn't quite make him fit, nor Darryl. Mr. Frank Lauser, reputedly of New

Jersey, was probably the "Frank" who Benson had breakfast with and, I was increasingly sure, the guy with the stun gun in the forest. I tried it on different ways: Maybe two Subarus out that night, and Lauser was some innocent. Maybe Jeremiah had been hit by a drunk. Maybe some fan of *E. coli* had decided to get back at Jerry for his insulting the bugs in his stories.

But Darryl had trashed Jeremiah's trailer and had taken something from it. And I didn't see any clear picture emerging from my mentally jigsawing the case.

So I called another number, a secure unlisted line belonging to Sam Calloway of Denver, an old friend of John Lincoln's who had set up our Atlanta office with its own computer network and who had, just as a favor to John, hacked for us a startling volume of information from a dozen absolutely secure sites. He'd once been a cryptographer for the NSA, back when code breaking was a matter of people using machines instead of vice versa.

I didn't know how friendly Sam would be to me. John was the one who had tracked down Sam's son and had kidnapped him from a cult, before I became his partner. There had, I gathered from John's stories, been some unpleasantness. The cult leader had targeted John for assassination, but Sam had casually wiped out the organization's credit worthiness and had frozen the assets of four men who had profited from the cult's activities. John had visited the men and had explained that if they ever wanted access to their money again, perhaps a détente would be in order.

The actual cult leader died "tragically" a few days later, having fallen overboard from the group's yacht on a moonless night. The organization regrouped as a bona fide religion. It's still around, but now it makes its money from self-help CDs and books. "Violence," John had told me, "is the resort of weak minds. Go first for the wallet."

I wondered to what extent Jeremiah's death was involved with somebody's wallet.

Sam answered the phone as he always had: "Yah?" I imagined his bulk occupying its customary space with three or four computer screens spread around him. He was a wealthy man, and he loved his work. He had told John and me that his company earned over twenty million a year just from selling and placing ads on porn sites.

"Oakley here, Sam."

"Great to hear your voice! How are you? Where are you? I lost you after the funeral."

"Moved to Vermont. I'm taking a kind of sabbatical."

"You got me at a busy time, son. My server in Denmark has crashed, and I'm redirecting its traffic to a new one in Berlin." I heard the rattle of a keyboard. "Go ahead, though, I can talk."

"I need a favor. I'm looking for information on a Frank Lauser who I'm increasingly thinking was the man who tied a guy to a tree and tortured him with a stun-gun. And he's into something with another suspect in the killing of a friend of mine. I'm pretty sure about the guy and the tree, but the only link to Lauser is that he rented a car similar to one the torturer drove off in." I decided not to get into the breakfast with Benson.

"You got Internet access?"

"I don't have electricity."

"Weird. Or scary. Or maybe nice, depending. Wait a second."

More rat-a-tat of the keyboard, and then Sam said, "I think that's it. Let me switch machines. OK, give me the dope on your guy."

I told him that he had a New Jersey PO box but had been pulled over on the highway heading to Burlington, Vermont.

"OK. I got your guy's credit report, medical records, DMV information, some Social Security and tax stuff. He doesn't have a website of his own. His e-mail's through his cable company, meaning he's got a cable modem. Heavy use, I see. Maybe he downloads a lot of dirty movies. Hmm . . . no, his IP address isn't registered with any of the heavy porn sites."

"What solid info can you give me?"

"The guy is fifty-three years old, divorced . . . sheesh, four times, currently unmarried. Huh. Next time you see him, call him Dr. Lauser—PhD in organic chemistry. He lives in an apartment that rents for just short of four thousand a month."

"In Newark?"

"In Manhattan." He gave me an address on Seventy-Fifth Street. "He's got a PO box in Newark, too, the one you mentioned. Let's see. Uses his credit cards to the tune of six, seven grand a month, pays off the whole balance every month."

"Where does he work?"

"He seems to be living off investment income, some consulting work. Three times last year, one stint for seventy-five grand, one for fifty, one for one fifty-five, two different companies: Genotypes Consolidated and Alston Genetic Services. Wait a second. OK, Genotypes is out of Bonn, Germany, but they have offices and facilities in Cambridge, Mass. Alston's a US company, registered in Delaware. But Delaware companies make me suspicious. Most of the Fortune 500 are chartered there—easy incorporation rules. Alston doesn't seem to have any offices there, just a PO box. It's a shell company for something. OK, the stock is wholly owned by Matterhorn Research Inc., which is headquartered in the Bahamas. They're covering their tracks. Some American corporation will own all the stock in Matterhorn. Let me see, let me see . . . got it. Matterhorn is owned and controlled by a Vermont company, my friend. Benson Forestry Products. They paid Dr. Lauser seventy-five thousand last year for consulting services."

"How about the Bonn company? Any link?"

"Harder to tell. Germany's harder. Give me a day?"

"No, don't waste the time. This is enough to go on."

"Got lots more if you need it. He has seven fillings in his teeth, and his last colonoscopy was negative, but he's got a blood pressure problem and his cholesterol's worse than mine. He's on a beta-blocker. Maybe that's why he's divorced, that stuff can give a man erectile dysfunction."

"Do me a favor and never check me out."

"Oh, son, somebody's probably checked you out thousands of times. This is the information age. Hang on a sec. OK, with this Benson Forestry, the CEO is Caleb Benson, the vice president and secretary-treasurer is Eva Benson. Caleb owns forty-three percent of the stock, the rest is in the hands of other relatives—at least they're all named Benson—but Eva's the only other Benson official in Vermont. Hmm. She doesn't own any stock that I can see, though. Company reported a loss last year, which was picked up by D&B. They're liquid about a quarter of a million, in four banks, three in the US. They've been on a downhill slide for three out of the last four years, in fact. Trees not selling for much up there?"

"I haven't kept track. What can you give me on Benson?"

"You are a busy man. OK, let me see. Benson personally was doing OK until two years back. His salary was four hundred thousand a year, plus bonuses that just about doubled that. The corporation was paying dividends up to four years ago. Bad year, then a so-so one, then two bad ones in a row. Last year was the worst, a substantial posted loss, no dividends.

Caleb took a salary cut and . . . but wait, he put Eva on the payroll. So Caleb netted about two hundred and thirty grand, and Eva just about the same. I'll bet they have some pissed-off relatives."

"What does the company actually do?"

"Timber, it says here, and they hold about twelve thousand acres in Vermont and New Hampshire as assets. They don't have a website."

"A bad year, but they hired Lauser to be a consultant to the tune of seventy-five thousand?"

"Twice."

"Can you find any connection between Benson's holdings and Native American tribes?"

"What? Wait, let me scan. No, nothing. But I'll check one of the services with a cross-search. 'Benson Forest Products,' 'Native American.' Guess I should throw in 'Indian' as a search term too."

"And Abenaki." I spelled it for him.

I heard Sam typing again, and he hummed a snatch of "Moonlight in Vermont."

"Stop it," I said. "You'll give me an earworm."

"Nice song. I like the Ella Fitzgerald–Louis Armstrong version. Son of a bitch, I got a hit. Two years ago next month one of the Benson crews was bulldozing a skidder trail—whatever the hell that is—through the woods. They unearthed some human bones. Turned out to be eight-hundred-year-old bones, from an Abenaki burial site. Vermont made them stop work. OK, follow it up . . . says here the Abenaki are raising money to relocate the bones to a burial site up north, or else they want to buy the land from Benson and rebury the bodies there. No resolution, they may still be negotiating."

A connection at last. "OK," I said. "Can you find anything on what Benson's genetics company is doing?"

"OK. This is becoming one big favor, Oakley."

"I'll pay for your time."

"Don't insult me. Hmm. Sorry, but I don't think I can help you. The company never issued any press releases, never did anything other than file tax returns. They don't have a listed phone number. You can't prove by this they're even in the genetics business. What the hell, it's the last great unregulated frontier. Any schmuck can set up a lab to do gene splicing for a ten thousand dollar investment. No shortage of amateur experts out there. Sometimes an entrepreneur will hit it lucky and sell something to a big corporation for mucho dinero. Monsanto bought the terminator technology from someone else."

"Guy in his basement?"

"Little bigger, but not much. Could've been a lone experimenter. Genetics experiments can be done by high school kids. You know, if you make food or chemicals or toys, the FDA or the FTC or some other agency will check to make sure your product isn't dangerous. But mess with the genetic code and nobody gives a damn, though it's potentially as destructive as making an atom bomb in your garage. If a gene jumps into the wild, it can change the ecosystem, the whole environment. Monsanto's engineered cotton and corn produces its own pesticide. What if flowering plants got that gene? What would happen to the bees? Mark my words, we're looking at the asbestos of the twenty-first century. One day we'll wake up and realize how dangerous genetic engineering is, and then we'll have to spend billions of dollars cleaning up."

I thought of something else. "Sam, one more thing. Can you pull medical records on Caleb and Eva Benson?"

"It'll take a minute." He started to hum again, stopped himself, and I listened to him breathe. Then he said, "Sorry, nothing. Either they're extraordinarily healthy, or else they pay cash for services. Or maybe they use phony names. Nobody ever checks, particularly if you pay up front for services, in cash." I heard more typing. "Just for fun, let me try criminal records. Nothing on Eva. Know her maiden name?"

"No."

"Richardson. Eva Marie Richardson. Born in Vermont, graduated from the University of Vermont, BS in business, went on for an MBA. Good grades. Uh-oh, naughty. One arrest for public drunkenness and lewdness."

"Lewdness?" I asked.

"Might have told a cop to perform an act of fornication upon himself. Might have been a reduced charge from prostitution. No media coverage. Happened in Albany, New York."

"Four hours away. Was she convicted?"

"No. Charges dismissed. Either it was a bad bust, or she had enough money for a good lawyer."

"How about Caleb?"

"Civil suit against him by the family of an ex-wife. Violation of her civil rights. Damn, it says they alleged that he killed her or had her killed. Hunting accident on his own land near the Canadian border. Hit in the head by a twelve-gauge slug. Never found the shooter or the gun, so when they tried to sue it went nowhere. But in the initial filing, the wife's family brought out stuff about Benson once setting somebody's car on fire. In his younger days he beat up some people pretty badly in barroom brawls. His witnesses say he's basically a good guy with a lousy temper. He took anger-management classes, yada yada. The suit was dismissed. With no smoking gun, there was no way to tie him to the death."

"How long after his wife's death did he marry Eva?"

"Four months. His grieving was perfunctory, I would say." More keyboarding. "And Eva had been married and divorced, too. Her husband, Anthony J. Goodwin, had been arrested for possession of a little more than a kilo of uncut heroin. That's a damn big drug bust for Vermont. Goodwin claimed it must have been planted, he had no involvement with drugs, didn't use them, but he copped a plea and drew a minimum seven-year sentence in a prison in upstate New York. He was busted near Fort Ticonderoga. Two months before Eva married Caleb. He was arrested a week after Benson's wife died. Eva got an uncontested divorce from him six weeks later. And then two weeks after that she marries Caleb. This was eight years ago."

I had been idly sorting through the files that lay beside me on the bed. I sat up straight, holding one. "Sam, can you find me the phone number for Genotypes Consolidated?"

"California, Massachusetts, or Bonn?"

"Massachusetts."

"No problemo." He read me the number and I copied it down. I thanked him and got off the phone.

I dialed Genotypes Consolidated and, as expected, got the standard voicemail routine. I left a message asking Dr. Frank Lauser to call me at his earliest convenience.

Then I tried his Manhattan number. I heard his professor-like voice on an answering machine, telling me I knew what to do when I heard the beep.

After the beep, I said, "Frank, if you're there, pick up. We need to talk about seventy thousand volts in the forest." Nobody picked up. I left my name and number.

20

I was pondering my next move when yellow light flicked across the front window, light that shouldn't have been there. I rolled off the bed and grabbed my jacket. The gun was still in the pocket and, remembering, I pulled a box of bullets from the dresser under my washbasin and replaced the spent round that'd bravely taken out a headlight.

I doused the kerosene lantern and ducked out the door and headed down the trail to the road. Below on the old logging road, headlights jolted and jounced as someone took the route at no more than five miles per hour.

It was a shiny new Mercedes, dark gray in the moonlight. I half-crouched behind my Jeep. The driver killed the engine, and when the interior light came on, I recognized Eva Benson. I stood and said, "Hello again."

She was startled. "You're Oakley Tyler," she said. "You came to my house."

"That's right, Mrs. Benson."

"I need to talk with you."

"So talk."

"Can't we go inside?" I could see her only as a darker

silhouette against the gray background of moonlit snow. "I don't like it out here."

"Come on, then. Watch your step." She took my arm and I led her back up the hill. I asked, "Are you alone, or is someone else going to show up?"

"All alone. You, too?"

"No. There's a bear."

"What?" Her grip tightened.

"He's not around at the moment." We got to the cabin and I asked her to wait until I had a light on. Inside I tossed the top part of the blanket down to cover the file contents spread on my bed, then struck a match and lit the kerosene lantern. Eva stepped inside, looking around, surveying the cabin with a sort of interior decorator avidity. I picked up the half glass of wine I had left by the bed and said, "Care for a drink?"

"What are the choices?"

"Red wine, vodka, melted snow."

"What's the red wine?"

I picked up the bottle and read the label. "A 1998 Coteaux-du-Languedoc, Château Véronique. Certified organic."

"Wonderful." She sat at the table, and her blonde hair swayed around her face. "I could use a drink after today." I poured one for her and she sampled it, pronouncing it to be very good.

"Glad you approve." I took the bentwood rocker. "Why do we need to talk, Mrs. Benson?"

"I want to know what's going on, why you came to the house. You've been asking people around town about us. Is Caleb in some kind of trouble?"

"I think you'd be the first to know."

"It's warm in here." She unzipped her coat and pulled it open. She was wearing a pale brown cashmere sweater, eloquent of money and sex appeal.

"Why do you think your husband may be in trouble?" I asked.

She sipped her wine. "He often is. It's not as bad lately, but he has a temper, and he's such a big hulk of a man."

"Where is he now?"

"I haven't seen him for two days." She gave me a kind of hurt look, as though I were responsible. "He had a meeting in town, and then he went off surveying some of his land. He's done this before, taken off and not let me know where he's going. His secretary can get in touch with him, but I can't."

She said it with such bitterness that I asked, "Something going on between them?"

"One could assume that. She may be in line for my job." She drank more wine. "Wife, I mean. Tell me what's going on. Caleb's been acting odd for nearly two years. What has he done?"

"I don't know." I raised my glass and from behind it, watching her closely, I said, "It may have something to do with Jerry Smith."

She snorted an unladylike burst of laughter. "Jerry Smith is a total nerd."

"But he's involved somehow. And a man named Frank Lauser."

"I don't know him," she said too quickly.

"Yes, you do. Your company hired Lauser twice in the last year as a consultant."

She sprang up from her chair. "How did you find that out?"

"It's publicly available information. What did your company hire Lauser to do?"

"I don't know."

"Come on. You're an officer of the corporation."

"You don't know much about how a business works. I have the title of VP, but absolutely zero responsibilities or powers."

"You're also secretary-treasurer. You must have signed Lauser's paychecks."

She shook her head. "I sign whatever our CPA hands me. Did your informant tell you I have no stock ownership? That means no input."

"Yet you were paid a salary of two hundred and thirty thousand last year."

"Why are you doing this?" She collected herself and sat down again. "Look, you're acting like we've broken the law. We haven't. Our company is trying to improve the environment. We're planting new trees where loggers once were clear-cutting. We're the good guys. What are you trying to do to us?"

"I'm just trying to find out who killed Jeremiah Smith."

"That was a hit-and-run accident. I didn't have anything to do with it, and Caleb didn't either."

"And Caleb doesn't have any problem with the Abenakis."

"Look, that's completely different. If those people get tribal status, a lot of landowners are going to be burned, not just Caleb. Those people want us to hand Vermont over to them."

"It used to be theirs."

"Not anymore. Do you know your history? The Abenaki fought the American settlers in the French and Indian War. They lost, and we won. Isn't there something about victors and spoils?"

"Yet they were here first."

"That's—"

A loud banging on the door cut her off. She went pale. I jumped up and peeked through the door.

Wanda stood there, wearing a frayed red wool coat over a sweater and blue jeans. She said, "Oakley, I have to tell you about Darryl—"

She broke off, seeing Eva inside. "That's her car, then," she said. "What the hell is she doing here?"

"I was trying to find out."

"I know you," Eva said to Wanda. "The little girl from Northfield who shacked up with my husband when you were working at Santos' Bar in Montpelier."

Wanda pushed past me. "Listen, you, that's a lie! I told him I wasn't for sale or for rent. Something you wouldn't have thought to tell him."

Eva stared at her stone-faced. "He took you to a hotel."

"Jesus Christ!" Wanda leaned on the table. "I was married and working my way through college. I delivered a two-hundred-dollar bottle of champagne to your husband's hotel room. I was there for maybe one full minute."

Eva began, "That's bullshit—"

Something thudded heavily against the back wall of the cabin, making the whole place vibrate for a second, as though a bolt of lightning had hit nearby.

I blew out the kerosene lamp just as the side window gave a sharp crack and I heard the dull chunk of a slug embedding itself in one of the beams on the other side of the room. I grabbed my jacket, found the pistol, and ordered, "Down on the floor, and lie flat."

I pulled my emergency flashlight from beside the bed. "Stay away from the door," I said. "Wanda, did you see or hear anyone when you walked up here?"

"Deer on the edge of the forest."

"How many cars?"

"Your Jeep, the Mercedes, mine."

"Stay put." I crawled to the door and pushed it slightly ajar. Nothing. I eased it open, hearing a hinge creak. It sounded as loud as a high trumpet note from Louis Armstrong. I wormed out onto the narrow porch. A long way down the trail I saw a flicker of light, as if someone had turned on a flashlight to get his bearings.

I jumped up and ran, following the edge of the forest. I could hear someone blundering through the increasingly slushy snow downhill. I didn't know if there were two of them or only one. I heard a car door slam down at the bottom of the logging road, then the roar of the engine starting, but by the time I made it down, whoever it was had already gone.

I slogged back to the cabin. Wanda was sitting on the floor; Eva had rolled over to my mattress on the floor. I closed the door and said, "I think it's safe. He drove away." As they got up, I lit the kerosene lantern again, but kept it low.

"Who was it?" Wanda asked, standing up.

"I don't know. Whoever it was must have come right behind you. You sure you weren't followed?"

"I don't know. I wasn't expecting anyone to follow me."

Eva was visibly upset. "I'm leaving." She pushed herself up from the bed.

"But Wanda will have to back her car out for you to get past."

Wanda had a small flashlight in the pocket of her coat. The two women followed its feeble beam downhill while I took a look at the roof beam where the bullet was lodged, and tried to judge where the shooter might have been. Then I made my way around back. Snow had piled high at the left corner of the house. I saw tracks and bent down to study them.

Wanda came around the corner, nearly making me draw my pistol before I realized it was her. "What is it?"

I shone the light on the deep footprints.

She said, "Damn, that's a bear." She pointed to a dark hank of hair caught in one of the rough-hewn boards. "There's where he bumped the cabin. Must have been a poacher after him, took a wild shot."

"No," I said. "The guy parked at the bottom of the road. He came up the hill. He wouldn't have seen anything behind the cabin, not even something big as a bear."

We went back inside, and hung blankets over the front and side windows. Wanda said she didn't feel safe sitting in a chair, so we sat cross-legged on the floor, leaning against the north and east corner walls. Her eyes glittered in the faint lamplight. "Relax," I said. "Nobody could aim at us without coming in through the door."

"You think it was Darryl, don't you?"

"It's possible."

"No. He would have seen my car. I really don't think he would have shot, knowing I was inside. It had to be somebody after the bear, or you. Or that Benson bitch. Was she trying to bed you?"

"She didn't give me the come hither treatment. I think she wanted just what she told me—to find out why I'm asking about her husband." I studied Wanda's face. "Did Caleb Benson try to put a move on you?"

"Oh, boy. Maybe three hundred times."

"Did you see much of him?"

"Enough. He came into the bar once or twice a week when he was in town. I knew a girl who said yes to him once. She left town soon after."

"So why did you come, Wanda? You said it was about Darryl."

"Just to tell you to lay off. He's OK. He may be a lazy shit, but he's harmless. He tries to do the right thing."

"But he used to beat you up."

"No! What gave you that idea?"

"The night you went bowling, you said it was tough on a woman when a man slapped her around."

She exhaled. "Oh, hell, I wasn't talking about Darryl. That was Marie's dad, a boy named Phil Newton. He was insecure and jealous because we were both in college at the same time and I had higher grades, believe it or not. He slapped me around once, and I warned him. The second time I took Marie and left."

"So Darryl was an improvement."

"He tried to treat me well. But Darryl couldn't hold a job. Smoked a lot of dope, that kind of thing. Not exactly a good father figure."

"And not a good husband for you."

"I don't know. I could have put up with him if was just the two of us, I guess. Maybe try to straighten him out. And he liked Marie. Used to carry her around on his shoulders. She liked him too, and she'd obey him when she wouldn't obey me." She had picked up a leaf that one of us must have tracked in. It was wet but brittle, and she crumbled it. "I just don't want Darryl to go to jail, that's all. He's not a bad man."

"He shot out the taillights on my Jeep."

"And you shot his truck, I heard."

"Do you know where he was last night?"

"No."

"I think he might have been standing guard in the woods with a rifle while another man tortured Jerry Smith with a stun gun."

"What?"

"And this morning I caught him and Bill Grinder on my land, both of them armed."

"Darryl hunts," she said.

I plowed ahead: "Not long after that he drove to Jeremiah Smith's trailer, entered it illegally, and went through it pretty thoroughly."

"Are you sure?"

"I have a good eyewitness."

"He must be in trouble, doing stuff like that." She shook her head. "Damn. Look, will you help him? As a favor to me?"

"Not if he helped kill Jeremiah."

"That was an accident."

"No." I grinned without mirth. "It was no boating accident. And it wasn't a shark. It was someone committing murder, and the weapon was a vehicle with out-of-state plates."

"Huh?"

I said, "Pop culture references are lost on you. But what I said is true: someone killed Jeremiah. I thought so at the time, and now I'm positive. Caleb Benson's in on it somehow, and Bill Grinder. And Darryl."

"Darryl's scared," Wanda said. "I called him after I heard about the shooting. He wouldn't talk to me. He still tries to get me to take him back, but I can tell something's bothering him, something big. Maybe Bill got him involved in something crooked, I don't know. Darryl's worked part-time for Bill off and on for years, but a part-time mechanic doesn't get the kind of money Darryl's been spending around town. He paid Bobby Dominey cash for that truck of his. He never had that kind of money in his life."

"He smokes pot. Does he deal it?"

"I'd have heard, and he'd have had to get half the town stoned to make the kind of money he seems to have. I thought he might be smuggling something in or out of Canada, but I don't know what."

"It would be a stupid racket for him to try."

"Yeah, well, he hasn't won any Rhodes scholarships." She got to her knees, then to her feet. "I'd better go. The neighbor lady is watching Marie. Walk me to my car?"

I picked up the flashlight. On the way down I studied the snow, but the warming weather had reduced it to slush that wouldn't hold a good footprint. As Wanda backed out to the road, I considered going into town and renting a motel room. But if someone sincerely wished me dead, I'd be no safer there.

I turned off the flashlight and gave myself a moment for my eyes to adjust, then made my way back uphill. Outside the cabin, I paused. "Thank you, Grandfather," I said loudly.

The great night brooded silently.

I went inside and closed the door. I was down to my last bottle of wine.

As I opened it, I saw that the corner of the blanket on my bed had been thrown back. The files were missing.

Curiouser and curiouser, as Alice had said. I would have to do something about this.

But first I had to do something about that last bottle of wine.

21

The phone shrilled me out of sleep. Thinking it was still night, I fumbled for it, and then as I registered the leak of daylight around the blanket covering the front window I realized the sun was well up. "Tyler here."

"Mr. Tyler." The voice was familiar, but I couldn't quite place it. It had the Vermont accent. Then it clicked.

"Mr. Benson," I said. "I tried to reach you at your office."

"I was checking some land," he said.

"See anyone tied to a tree?"

He grunted. "I don't want to talk on the phone. Can we meet this afternoon? Do you know Burlington?"

"Just where it is." It was an hour west of me, on the eastern shore of Lake Champlain.

"There's a place there called the Five Spice Café." He gave me the street address. "You can Google it," he added.

"No, I can't. No computer."

"Oh?" He sounded surprised. "Well, just stop and ask. You can find Church Street easily enough, and anybody along there will know where it is. Meet me there at one-thirty."

"I could just come to your place, or you could come here."

"No. People talk. I don't want locals to see me with you."
He paused. "You're wondering if I killed Jeremiah Smith. I
didn't."

"Then who did?"

"That's what we can talk about. At one-thirty."

"What time is it now?"

He sounded irritable. "God's sake, you don't have a computer, don't you even have a watch? A clock?"

"No."

"Seven thirty-seven AM," he said, and hung up just as I
remembered my phone would tell me the time.

I climbed out of bed and took the blankets off the windows. The slug had left a spider-webbed round hole in one
pane. Outside, the sky was making the change from rosy pink
to china blue. High cirrus clouds brushstroked it like a delicate
painting. Through the window I saw rivulets of water running.
The eaves wore beards of dripping icicles.

The cabin was cold enough to make me hurry to get the
fire going. A quart of lukewarm water remained in the cast-
iron snowmelt pot atop the stove. I used it for a sponge bath.
Then I dressed and went back to the spot where the bullet had
buried itself in a two-by-six roof joist. I pulled my sturdy table
over and stood on it, eyes level with the hole in the wood, and
sighted through the hole in the window. The shooter had been
near the edge of the clearing east of the cabin, unless he'd
been hiding sniper-fashion in the treetops farther downslope.

When I stepped out the air was crisp, not freezing, and
it smelled fresh with pine sap. A lot of snow will melt today,
I thought. The temperature probably was right around forty
and might climb into the fifties with full sun. I couldn't make
anything of the tracks, not even in daylight. Too much slush.

I walked as far as the rock outcrop, half expecting to see Sylvia, but only an outspoken chipmunk waited there, chittering at me from a cleft in the rocks to go away and leave him alone. I wondered if she'd be up Route 12 near the tree I was supposed to visit this morning.

I drove out there in the Jeep, through a fair amount of traffic. A guy tailgating me slammed on his brakes when I slowed to make the turn onto the abandoned logging trail. This time no deer were there to direct me, and maybe my turn was a little abrupt. I found the spot where the Subaru had parked. From the ruts in the muddy slush, it looked like someone had driven in and out several times in the last few days. I found the spot where I had first seen Jerry tied to the tree, then in the daylight saw I had missed an easy descent that I could have taken in the darkness.

As Sylvia had instructed me, I stood at the tree, facing east, and raised my right arm out to my side. I took off on foot, following the rolling terrain. Far ahead one dead tree towered above the rest of the forest. I caught occasional glimpses of it. My path was taking me more or less straight toward it. It served as an aid to navigation. I hit the overgrown old logging trail again and saw more fresh tracks. Hard to tell, but it looked like two different vehicles, the deeper tracks from a tire tread with a diamond pattern.

And then I emerged in a churned-up clearing. The vehicles, or at least one of them, had been in and out of here repeatedly and had turned around many times. Along the margin were boot tracks and drag marks. The boot tracks looked about size nine. I thought of Darryl and his truck and wondered about the tires he ran on it.

Brown twigs with brittle pine needles littered the pathway. I followed it along deeper into the forest. Then I came out in a

much larger clearing, an acre or more, and found an expanse of
small pine-sapling trunks, all cut off about six inches from the
ground. From the sawdust, it looked as though the trees had
been trimmed off by a handsaw, not a chainsaw, which mostly
only leaves chunks. Most of the stubs were between an inch
and two inches in diameter, the same size as the brush Darryl
had been burning.

I scouted around the clearing. On the far side I sighted back
toward the trail I'd followed coming in, then across the forest
in the opposite direction, more or less south. I came across
some weathered boot tracks in the snow, not the same size as
the ones I'd followed in. They seemed to belong to someone
doing the same thing I was, scoping out the clearing. I made a
complete circuit.

I saw another, smaller clearing below and walked down to
it. More small pine stumps, but these were gray and weathered,
not fresh. They bordered a small wash that in wet weather was
probably a brook. I followed the gully for a hundred feet or so
and found a few more stumps. Then fifty more feet brought
me to a stand of small pines among the hardwood. There were
only three, none more than three feet tall, and all were dead,
needles a rusty brown, like the saplings I had seen in Darryl's
pickup. I flexed a small branch on one and it snapped in my
hand, with no give at all.

Something interesting. I climbed back uphill, then back-
tracked to my Jeep.

Back in Northfield I visited City Hall and found the town
clerk's office. A soft-spoken middle-aged woman with a June
Cleaver look told me it was indeed possible to discover who
owned any given parcel of land within the jurisdiction. She
took me into a room with a battered library table occupying
most of the floor space and pulled out a set of plat maps that

she thought would show the area I described. As far as I could tell from distances and the landmark of a brook that had to be the one I had discovered, the land made up one parcel of something more than four hundred acres. It was owned by Benson Forestry Products Inc.

I went back to the Jeep and called the number for *This Week*. The guy with the ponytail answered, and I identified myself and asked for Gina.

"Oh, right, the gumshoe," the man said in an exceptionally maladroit Bogart impression. In his normal voice, he said, "Hang on."

Gina took half a minute to pick up, and then she said, "Hello, Tyler. Or should I call you the Casanova of Northfield?"

"I'd say that was an overstatement."

She laughed. "Wanda's an old friend. She's written for the paper now and again, and I'd like her to do more of that. She's busy being a mom and waitress, though." She laughed. "And news does get around. How did it feel having two wild women in your cabin at the same time?"

I had to grin. "Honest to God, I don't see why you even bother to publish a newspaper. By the time it hits the streets everyone knows everyone else's business anyway."

"Well, there's only a half-million people in the state, lots of us are related to each other, and most of the others are friends. Look, we're a week from the next deadline, but that doesn't mean I have time to chat about this and that. What's on your mind?"

"I need somebody to tell me about genetic engineering."

"Don't know anything about it except what I've read in the papers. It's either going to feed the world or end life as we know it, or maybe both. Ask Jerry, he's the one who wrote all the stories. But be aware that he's very anti–big business. I think he's sore because he didn't get a job."

"I don't understand."

"While he was still working on his dissertation. He interviewed in New York, New Jersey, Connecticut, but he hadn't finished that PhD and nobody wanted to hire him."

"He told me he was going to finish his degree soon."

"Maybe. He had a setback when his major professor at UVM died a while back. They thought it was some bizarre seizure, but it turned out he poisoned himself somehow, picked some toxic mushrooms or something. People do that all the time here—couple of times a year, anyway. Get some wild mushroom book and go out in the woods and try to make a gourmet meal out of something deadlier than blowfish."

"I hadn't heard. Anyway, Jerry's touchy with me. I need someone else to bring me up to speed."

"Let me think. There's Nigel Jameson. Retired UVM professor. Jerry used him as a source in some of his stories. British guy, old but sharp as a pin. I can find his number. Hey, would there be a story in this?"

"Not if you leave crime to the dailies."

"We could make an exception. Jameson's asked that we not give out his number. Let me call him and then call you back."

"That'll do, thanks."

———◆———

She called back in less than five minutes. "OK, twenty minutes from now, his place. Pick me up?"

"I'm on the road now."

"How close?"

"Not long."

"Meet you on Main Street in front of the building. Do you know where Jerry is?"

"Haven't spoken to him since yesterday. Is he missing?"

"I wouldn't call it that, but he missed a deadline and I had to throw something else into the space. He's not answering his phone."

I didn't have any response to that. "See you soon," I said.

A few minutes later I picked her up and she directed me to a house that looked as though it had been plucked from *The Arabian Nights* and plunked down in Vermont. It was a yellow Gothic on a hilltop just a little south of town, all steep rooflines and nine-foot-all diamond-pane windows. I stopped in the drive and we walked across a flagstone court-yard. Jameson met us at the door, a man with the rumpled, tweedy look of the absent-minded professor. His thinning white hair had been carefully arranged on the pink dome of his scalp. His face was dominated by a potato nose and framed by oversized ears. He had the droopy brown eyes of a basset hound. I gathered he was in his seventies, but he stood perfectly erect and gave me a firm handshake. Then he kissed Gina on the cheek.

"Come in, come in," he said. "Gina, it's perfectly wonder-ful to see you again. And this young man is a detective, is he?"

"Well, I have been, sir," I said. "My name's Oakley Tyler."

"Oh, heavens, don't call me 'sir.' Not until they knight me. And that may happen one day, should my work come to the attention of Her Majesty." He chuckled at his own mild joke.

He saw us into a cluttered parlor. The walls themselves, hung with oil paintings, bore elaborate murals, clouds and angels on the ceiling. He had set out a teapot and three cups. "Now," he said, passing each of us a cup of tea and offering a small plate of ginger snaps, "you wish to know something about genetic engineering. I'm not really an expert on that, though I try to keep up with current research as reported in the journals. But I will do my best to help you. What, in particular, do you want to know?"

"I want to know about the possibility of genetically modifying pine trees," I told him.

"Possibility? What can I say? Not only is such engineering possible, my dear young man, it has been done. Many companies are working to improve forestry products. Pine is one of the primary raw materials for construction and paper. It is one of the fastest-growing softwoods as well. Oh, my, yes, the pine can certainly lend itself to genetic engineering. It isn't particularly difficult. A lab could be set up in a space no larger than my kitchen. The complexity of genetic engineering lies in the organisms in question, not in the equipment. It isn't a task on par with splitting the atom."

"Why would someone genetically engineer the trees, though? What would they hope to do?"

"Heavens, any number of possibilities. The Southern Pine Beetle is a major problem in pulpwood production. Perhaps someone would try to engineer pines that do not attract these creatures. Or it could be that someone would want to make pines mature in less time than it takes them naturally. That would have applications in, oh, reforesting an area hit by a bad wildfire, for example."

I handed him a small sprig of pine, the one I'd picked up at Darryl's. "Could you tell anything from that?"

He took it. "It's a dead pine twig." He broke one of the brown needles and sniffed it. "It still has some flowing resin in it, so it hasn't been dead for more than a month or two. I think this particular pine may have died from a fungal infection, something that's called rust. It's a common problem for pines. The tree is infected, the fungus spreads, the needles turn brown, and the tree dies."

"Could this be from a genetically engineered pine?"

"That's possible. Did the tree die before this branch was cut?"

"I think so. I saw another tree about the same size, dead but standing, and it looked the same."

He shrugged. "Well, if it's part of a breeding experiment, it's a failure. When you try to produce a new variety of plant, whether by hybridizing, mutagenesis, or genetic modification, one goal—perhaps the primary goal—is the survivability of the product."

"A lot of trees like this were dead."

"A larger failed experiment, then. But of course a hundred other things could have killed it besides faulty genes: the wrong soil chemistry, herbicides, insects, drought—or excessive moisture. Climate extremes at the wrong point in the growing cycle. Have you ever gardened?"

"Not seriously."

"If you had, you'd know there are dozens of things that can kill a plant. You say there were many of these trees?"

"Maybe a hundred or more."

He frowned. "Scattered in the forest, or all together?"

"At least one large stand of them. I found a few stragglers in the woods among hardwoods. I was wondering if they might have died because of genetic modification, and if they had, whether the faulty gene might have jumped into the wild."

"Hmm. How big were the trees?"

I held my hand out. "No more than this tall, and none were more than two inches in diameter at the base."

"Then it's probably impossible that any faulty gene has escaped. Pines don't reproduce until they're from six to eight years old. The size you describe means these were probably no more than three. Did any of them have cones?"

"Not that I saw."

"Then you can rule out gene-jumping."

Jameson had laid the twig down, and Gina picked it up. I said, "Dr. Jameson, could you imagine any reason why someone might commit a crime to cover up a failed genetic-engineering experiment, if that's what this was?"

He patted down his white hair. "There are legal penalties for releasing genetically modified organisms into the environment without proper permits. I'd say the economic impact would be greater. If a company fails at an experiment, especially if that failure involves a violation of the law, the company loses the confidence of shareholders."

"Could that be serious enough to lead someone to torture or kill a man?"

"Who can say?" He sighed. "Mr. Tyler, the history of science is littered with the corpses of innovators. Marie Curie discovered radium, and the discovery cost that young woman her life. Galileo published his discoveries, and that cost him his freedom. However, crime is hardly a norm in scientific inquiry."

"What if a company were trying to design a better pine tree but screwed it up and created one that self-destructs after a couple of years?"

"A failure, but hardly dangerous. Any organism that destroys itself before reaching sexual maturity represents no threat to the environment. It takes itself out of the equation."

I finished my cup of tea, thinking hard. Say these were the trees Darryl had been burning—destroying the evidence of a failed experiment. Jeremiah might have come across the stand of dead trees and learned or guessed what had happened. He'd investigated as much as he could, maybe helped along by his grandson's newspaper stories and expertise.

So say Benson had tried and failed to create some super-pine. The effort flopped, and to protect his company, Benson was having the evidence burned. But Jeremiah had raised questions, had appeared on Benson's radar, and somehow Benson had decided to have him killed—or Frank Lauser had taken it on himself. Henry II, according to his own story, once irritably growled, "Will no one rid me of this meddlesome priest?" and some of his knights, taking that for an order, had ridden down to Canterbury and had stabbed an unarmed Thomas à Becket to death as he celebrated Mass in the cathedral. I could see Benson having Jerry tortured, or Lauser doing it, to learn how much Jeremiah might have told him.

But Dr. Jameson had just about convinced me that there was no need, no motive. I said, "I'm trying to see if the crime could be tied in with these dead trees."

Jameson smiled. "My dear fellow, you are the detective. Such questions are rather beyond my field."

I said slowly, "I believe it must have something to do with 'interfering.'"

He raised his white eyebrows high. "Oh?"

"Interfering with one form of life in a way that puts other life at risk."

"You may have a point," Jameson said. "In 1998 a company engineered a bacterium, *Klebsiella planticola*, so it would eat cellulose and excrete alcohol. That's a common soil bacterium, so common that virtually every plant species ever tested has shown up with it on their roots. The notion was to use the bacteria to decompose plant residue left in the field after harvest. Burning produces pollution. So a bug that ate the cellulose seemed a good bet: pile up the corn stalks or whatever, pack them in drums, toss in some *Klebsiella*, and in a few weeks you'd have sludge and alcohol. The sludge would contain the micronutrients and minerals and could be spread on the fields as fertilizer. In theory, the bacteria would die off as the process was completed, so it would self-destruct. But at the last minute, a smart young man at a college in Oregon asked, 'What would happen if the *Klebsiella* were still alive in the sludge?'"

"And?"

"And this bright young man experimented, and sure enough, sufficient *Klebsiella* remained active that plants fertilized with it were poisoned in a stew of alcohol from their own dissolving roots. Had that bacterium escaped into the wild, there are some who say it could have destroyed all plant life on Earth." He shuddered. "But a bacterium is a long way from a pine tree."

"Or a mushroom?"

He frowned. "Mushrooms?"

"I noticed three of them in the home of the man I believe was murdered. It's a long shot, but could this all be about mushrooms and not pines?"

"I don't know about murder, but mushrooms could contribute to the death of the pines. You see, pines are one of only three species of trees that require fungi to live. A fungus grows around the roots of pines, surrounding them, creating an intricate weblike network in the soil. This fungus—called mycorrhizae—actually sends tendrils into the roots of the tree, and it transports minerals, nutrients, and water directly into the roots. In exchange, the tree shares with the fungus some of the sugars it produces. It's a symbiotic relationship. Without mycorrhizae, pines die or else do very poorly. Forestry companies sell mycorrhizae and nematodes that support the growth of trees."

"Are there bad ones?" I asked.

He looked up into the far corner of the ceiling, where cherubs gazed back at us. "Indeed there are, bad at least for pines. The single largest living organism on Earth is a parasitic fungus out west, in Oregon, I believe, or perhaps Washington State. It's called *Armillaria*, and weighs hundreds of thousands of tons, may be eight thousand years old, and covers nearly ten square kilometers."

"What if the fungus, not the trees, had been genetically altered?"

"That could be problematic. If you created mycorrhizae that transported twice the usual nutrients and water into a pine tree, theoretically the tree would grow faster. But in nature nothing is ever free—there is always a trade-off. Enhance one quality and lose another. A change will always have unintended consequences. Always. For example, in addition to providing nutrients, mycorrhizae also protect the pine from other fungi that can attack the roots and cause them to rot. A pumped-up mycorrhiza might just lose that protective ability. And it could spread rapidly."

"How?"

"The mushrooms you mention. No doubt you have seen what are called fairy rings, circles of mushrooms, after heavy rains?"

"Yes."

"Actually the mushrooms are merely the visible reproductive system of a much larger organism that occupies the whole space within the circle, but underground, there's a network of tendrils intertwined with and interpenetrating the pine tree roots. The mushrooms produce spores, the spores spread on the wind, which is the main way the fungus reproduces. If the mycorrhizae were genetically engineered and faulty, its DNA could spread to other colonies of the same fungus, and its genetic code could replace that of the natural organism. In the most extreme case, it could destroy every pine tree in the world."

22

After dropping off Gina, I drove to Burlington trying to piece it all together. Benson had the scientific background, but so did the guy with the stun gun, the consultant Dr. Lauser. I tried it this way and that. Benson had tinkered with engineering a fungus, it went bad, and Jeremiah had stumbled across evidence that Benson's company had broken the law, or worse, that it had released something into the wild that threatened to kill off an economically important tree. On Benson's orders, someone had blown up Jeremiah's truck, had shot at him, and then had killed the old man. Maybe Lauser's consulting retainers included little chores like torturing Jerry to find out if his grandfather had tipped him off about the whole sorry business.

It was like trying to assemble a jigsaw puzzle that had been soaked in ink, with some pieces missing and some nothing more than soggy black pulp. I got to the Five Spice Café a little early. It was an Asian fusion place with a great wine list. As I sat and waited for Benson to show up, I people watched and made up guesses about who people were, deep down inside, and what they were talking about over lunch.

One thirty came and went; I'd moved from people-watching to a copy of the *Burlington Free Press* that a young man at the table next to mine offered me when he finished eating and got up to leave. I ordered at two, and at two thirty I paid the check and headed home. An hour later I drove up the old logging road—by now it was more like the bed of a mountain stream, running with meltwater—and saw a forest green Land Rover parked just out of sight of the main road, a newer, top-of-the-line model. I got out and glanced through the window and saw mail on the front seat, a scattering of letters addressed to Benson Forestry Products Inc. I didn't know if Benson was waiting at the cabin to talk to me, sighting in on me through a telescope mounted atop a high-powered rifle, or setting fire to my home.

I left my car and threaded my way through the edge of the forest, on the same side where I'd first met Sylvia. I circled up the hill until I came within sight of the clearing. Nothing looked out of order. The thin wisp of smoke from the chimney was about what I would expect of a fire that hadn't been stoked in hours.

I approached the cabin from a blind quarter and leaned against the back wall, just listening. No sounds from inside. I followed the wall back to the south corner. And then my cell phone trilled.

I grabbed it and whispered, "Yeah?"

It was Wanda. "Oakley, Darryl's on his way. What'd you do to him?"

"Nothing. I haven't seen him."

"Who called him?"

"Not me."

"Don't hurt him," she said. She paused and added, "He has his rifle."

I thumbed the phone off and switched off its ringer. Beside the window, I shouted, "Benson? Caleb Benson?"

No response.

I crossed the porch and unlatched the door. I pulled the door open, flattening myself beside it, not standing in the obvious place. "Benson!"

No sound. Not even the quarrelsome chipmunk. But from the open door drifted the sharp scent of cordite and the reek of the spilled contents of bladder and bowels.

In the far corner, crumpled into the space next to my washstand, lay the man who had wielded the stun gun. Blood congealed around a dark half-inch diameter hole in his shirt just left-center of his chest. The wall and floor were splattered with blood and bits where the bullet had exited. On the floor between us lay my shotgun, pointing toward him like a death-seeking compass needle. A pair of my gloves, black leather, lay palm to palm beside the weapon.

I guessed from the state of the body that Dr. Lauser had been killed within the past hour. There was nowhere in the room anyone could hide. I turned my back on the dead man and went toward the door. As I opened it I heard the report of a rifle from outside, and a chunk of the door jamb flew loose. Not too far away I heard someone ratchet a fresh round into a bolt-action rifle.

I left the door ajar and dropped to a crouch, then crawled over to the bed and to the rear wall behind it. I unhitched the panel beside the wood stack, raised it enough to look out, and scanned the forest that began ten feet behind the cabin. Clouds were coming in, like an early twilight. Nothing moved. I wormed through the opening and dropped onto the ice-crust of snow that had lain in shadow twenty-four hours a day. I edged around, keeping to the cover of the forest fringe.

I couldn't spot anyone. I couldn't clearly see the trail. Retreating back into the forest, I skirted down toward the drive. The shadows had been blurred by the overcast, and the sun had slipped behind the mountain. I froze as I heard voices, a woman's and a man's. I couldn't make out the words, and so I crept forward again.

Then, so close that it spooked me, I heard Bill Grinder's voice: "I ain't heard nothing. Better go check it out."

The woman sounded like Eva Benson: "I don't think he's hit. He'll come out."

"He may have called the cops."

"Not him. I know the type. He'll want to know what's going on before he calls for help."

"Look, I thought this was like before, we were gonna catch him in the open, make it look like a hunting accident."

"I told you, it has to look like he and Frank shot each other."

I was no more than thirty feet away from them, fifteen feet above them on the hillside. Between us stood a scatter of bare hardwood, a tangle of brush, and an outcrop of granite. I guessed they had been there in ambush and had missed me because I'd come in from the far side of the drive. I edged onto the granite, keeping low.

"If he was still alive, he would've come out by now," Grinder said.

I was able to peep over the top of the outcropping of stone. They stood beneath an enormous old oak left over from the ancient times when Vermont was all hardwood forest. Grinder wore hunting clothes and carried a rifle with a scope. Eva had on black stretch pants and a black ski jacket.

Aiming my pistol at Grinder, I called out, "Put down the rifle, Bill, and—"

I'd never seen a man that big move so fast. He spun and fired from the hip, exploding a chunk of rock two feet from my head. I felt bites of stone chips in my cheek, and I dropped down. I gave a gargling, dying groan.

"You got him," I heard Eva yell.

Grinder came tearing around the base of the escarpment, saw me lying on my side, and fired again. I heard the flat *thap* of a slug passing inches from my ear. I shot downhill at close range. Grinder staggered, hit, but he jerked off one more shot, and my left shoulder flared with pain. I tumbled down the granite slope and lost my gun.

Something smacked the side of my head, stopping my tumble and making the world go loose and wavery. I explored the damage to my shoulder with my good hand. My jacket was soaked with hot blood. My Police Special lay down the slope, almost within reach. Grinder lay on his side, clutching his belly and groaning.

I crawled toward the gun, but before I reached it, Eva stepped over Grinder. She had an automatic, a small one, but it looked at me from a round and deadly eye. "Stop," she said.

"You're not going to shoot me," I told her.

"Why not? You kidnapped and killed my business associate. Then when Mr. Grinder and I tracked you down, you shot at us."

She raised the weapon. And then Sylvia's voice cut the wilderness apart: "No! I will not allow it!"

Eva spun. Sylvia stood in the center of the logging road. The gun in Eva's hand fired, and Sylvia pitched over backward, as though hit in the center of her chest. I made the last lurch, grabbed my weapon, and fired downhill until the gun was empty.

Everything had gone hazy. I staggered up, but I couldn't see Sylvia or Eva. I took a step and fell, then pushed up again. Grinder was on his knees, trying to use his rifle as a prop, as a crutch, to get to his feet. He was drooling blood, keening. I went past him, looking for Sylvia.

Then I saw Eva. She had backed down the slope. She raised her small pistol, shaking. I lurched toward her, determined to take her down.

A rifle fired. I saw Eva jerk, half turn, and fall. Darryl, I thought. I didn't wait. I staggered across the hill, to the place where Sylvia had stood. No sign of her. I called, "Sylvia," my voice tearing my throat. I caught sight of something crumpled and brown that looked like her buckskin clothes, and half-stumbled, half-crawled, to it.

It was a doe. She lay on her side on bloodstained snow, staring at me with great, frightened eyes. She moaned, then with a mighty heave, she rolled to her belly and stood on shaking legs. I saw the bullet wound just behind her right shoulder, in the ribs. She limped away, broke into a clumsy halting run, and vanished in the dim twilight.

23

A sharp pain in my shoulder roused me. I woke disoriented, wondering where I was: a room splashed in early daylight. Cheap paneled walls, yellow painted ceiling. Darryl Garret's living room. I sat up, dizzy, and swayed there a moment. I heard voices: Darryl, Wanda. I vaguely remembered a jolting ride in the bed of Darryl's truck to the emergency room.

I peeled back a four-inch pad of dressing and looked at the damage. My shoulder had the Frankenstein look of blood-black stitches. I remembered police asking me questions, then a lawyer showing up, one on retainer from Benson Forestry Products. They let me go.

I got into my jeans. Wanda came in and looked at me. "You gonna live?"

"Do I have a choice?"

"You could use a shower."

"Among a lot of other things."

"Don't get your stitches wet."

Breakfast made me feel moderately human again, eggs scrambled with onions and Cabot Vermont Sharp Cheddar.

Homemade bread with raisins and cinnamon. "What happened to Benson?" I asked.

Darryl said stone-faced, "He wasn't there."

"He had to be there."

"That's not what we heard from the cops," Wanda said. "They told us he wasn't there. He tried to get you on the phone to cancel out on your lunch appointment. Something came up. His lawyer has witnesses who place him twenty miles away at the time of the shooting."

"I see."

"You OK?" Darryl asked. "You were out of it last night, man. Talking about a woman and a deer."

"One of you drive me back to my cabin?" I asked.

Wanda shook her head. "It's a crime scene." She paused, then added softly, "They didn't find another woman, Oakley. If she'd been there they would have spotted her. Just three bodies."

"Damn lucky you weren't the fourth," Darryl added.

"You took out Eva?"

He didn't react.

"Thanks."

Darryl stared down at his plate. "I came to help Bill, not you."

"You were too late. Is he dead?"

"Died about two this morning, they say."

Wanda said, "Darryl told me you convinced the police that Eva had killed Jeremiah."

"I told them to check out her car for evidence."

"Because she had temporary tags?" Wanda asked.

"And she had a motive," I said. "Her husband was testing a genetically-engineered fungus to make pines grow faster. It turned out to be a monster. Instead of encouraging growth, it killed the trees off. Jeremiah found out about it and was about to blow the whistle on them. So Caleb hired Grinder to kill Jeremiah, but his bullet just missed. Then Eva ran Jeremiah down with her car. Once Jeremiah was gone, Grinder hired Darryl to clean up the trees."

Darryl nodded silently.

I said, "I think Eva got Frank Lauser to question Jerry Smith because he was pretty savvy about genetics and they thought he might have tipped his grandfather off or the other way around. Lauser was the man with the stun gun. Was that you with the rifle, Darryl?"

"I wasn't gonna shoot anybody," he muttered.

"So Eva got in touch with Lauser, who was probably supposed to help her overpower me. But she killed him and intended to kill me, too, making it look like a shootout between us. I think Eva was more nervous than her husband was about having the story of the fungus and the pines come out. The company was struggling, and Caleb wasn't the best of husbands. She wanted to come out of it with some money. She didn't like my snooping around, so she decided to eliminate me." I paused. "Or maybe she and Caleb together decided that. Or maybe Caleb saw a quick death for his wife as cheaper than a divorce action."

Darryl said, "But he was twenty miles away."

"Says his lawyer," I said. "What did you take from Jeremiah's place?"

"He'd dug up one of the pine trees, roots and all. I burned it."

"Why?"

"Grinder gave me five hundred dollars and told me to keep my mouth shut. There were some from the forest, too."

Wanda asked, "What are you going to do about Benson?"

"We'll see," I told her. "His business is collapsing." I thought of the conversation I'd had earlier in the day with Sam and said, "When this gets out—and it will—the whole thing will come down, and he'll go to prison. I doubt he'll get far before the feds find him, and they probably don't need help from me."

———————◆———————

The police turned me away from my own property. The uniformed officer at the bottom of the drive guessed they'd be finished by that evening. It was OK to take my Jeep.

I drove one-handed to Montpelier and spent some time talking to Gina Berkof. When I finished, I said, "So is it a story?"

"Benson isn't going to like it."

"Benson isn't going to have the power he once had. Anyway, it's important. Someone's going to have to dig up that whole area, take care of that fungus. It's bigger than Love Canal."

"I'll run the story in some shape or form. But I've got bad news for you. Eva Benson didn't kill Jeremiah. The night that happened she was in Brattleboro hosting a fundraiser for a gubernatorial candidate who's friendly to timber interests."

"Not possible."

"No, she was there." She tilted her head. "Maybe someone else was driving her car. Darryl?"

"I don't think so," I said. "Maybe Grinder. He knew which way Jeremiah was walking that night."

She nodded with her lips pressed thin.

"Have you heard from Jerry?" I asked.

"He called in. He's working on some kind of memorial service for his grandfather next week. He asked for time off."

"Thanks," I said and stood up, to the accompaniment of a pleasant little assortment of shooting pains. "Are you free for dinner by any chance?"

"No. I'm in a relationship and very happy," she said.

"I'm not making a pass. I just like talking to you. Why don't both of you come? I feel the need for company tonight."

She held the smile. "Let me see what Elaine says. If it works out, Dutch treat?"

"Sounds good." I checked that she still had my cell phone number and left.

The police had left my place when I got back to North-field. I didn't want to go into the cabin. I walked to the granite outcrop where I'd sat imagining a changed world with Sylvia. I sat there for a while in the afternoon sun. Then, like mist condensing from the air, a figure appeared in the shadow of the forest: a yearling deer, his head cocked to one side. When I moved to look at him he bolted into the brush.

"Sylvia," I said aloud, "I hope you're all right. Take care of her, Grandfather. She had a reason to interfere."

There are uncanny moments in life when the whole world seems a living, listening thing.

They always pass.

24

On the way back to Montpelier for dinner with Gina and Elaine, I stopped at the Backwoods Bookstore. Bernie sat behind his desk, with a mound of cigarette butts smoldering in the ashtray and another one between the middle and ring fingers of his left hand. He was reading an old John D. MacDonald novel in dog-eared paperback, but he dropped a bookmark into it when I came in.

"Butch Cassidy himself," he said.

I stared at him blankly.

"You haven't seen today's paper."

"I usually avoid them."

He picked up the front page of the *Montpelier Times Argus* and displayed it like a banner. FOREST SHOOTOUT, the headline screamed. FORMER PRIVATE DETECTIVE WOUNDED.

"You're famous. So if you're wounded, why are you walking around?"

"I was lucky," I said. "The bullet missed bone, just tore up skin and muscle."

"Hence the unsightly shoulder bulge," he said. "Says here three people were shot and killed on your property yesterday, and you claim another was wounded and disappeared. That the Indian woman you asked me about, the one who wears buckskins?"

"She's the one."

"I've asked around. Most people think you've been drinking too much. But there's a woman in town, claims to be an Abenaki, who says you saw a—" he closed his eyes. "Let me get this right, a *Nolka Alnôbak*."

"And what's that?"

"Miss Sarah—she's my informant—tells me that in old stories told by the old folks of her tribe, there are tales about beings who are deer-people. They look like deer, but can take human shape. Usually a *Nolka Alnôbak* is a woman. The forest people send one to the tribe when they need help. They appear as women because that way the young men will listen." He dragged on the cigarette. "*Nolka Alnôbak*. Deer-people."

"Deer-people," I said.

"They can't hold human shape for more than a few hours. There are tales of young men who would fall in love with one, and they'd lie down together, but next morning she'd be gone, with just deer tracks. There are tragic stories—warrior sleeps with a beautiful maiden, wakes in the morning, kills a deer, and it's the woman he slept with."

"My woman was human," I said firmly.

"All right," Bernie said. "And nobody else in town ever saw her or heard of her."

"I guess so."

He shook his head. "Life is strange, Oakley. The VC always believed the spirits of their departed ancestors were helping them. There were times when I'd swear they were right"

"Thanks anyway, Bernie."

"Wait," he said, leaning forward. "Miss Sarah wanted me to ask you a question. She said it's important. When these deer-people come to humans, it's to impart some great secret, to teach wisdom, to give a prophecy. Miss Sarah wanted to know what message the deer-people have for us."

"Don't interfere."

"Huh?"

"That's the message," I said, and left him looking bewildered.

———————◆———————

I went back to Jerry's apartment building. His door was locked, as I expected. I pulled from my pocket the one thing I'd retrieved from my cabin: a leather case containing a compact but useful array of lock picks.

The door opened into the living room of Jerry's obsessively neat apartment. I did a quick walk-through: empty. I looked out the living room window and saw the river. My shoulder was pounding, but I didn't want to take any painkillers. I stood at Jerry's bookcase and looked at his reading material: forestry management manuals, microbiology texts, a college-textbook-looking book titled *The Psychopathic Personality*, and paperback novels. He liked thrillers and stories about serial killers.

In the kitchen I found a small stack of papers on the table. Receipts from a funeral home for Jeremiah's cremation. An oversized brown manila envelope, fat with something. And I found the files that had been taken from my cabin. That put Jerry with Eva. Curiouser and curiouser.

In the bedroom I found that Jerry slept on a raised futon. A side table, a dresser with mirror, and a locked four-drawer file cabinet completed the furnishings. A framed diploma on the wall averred that Jerry had graduated from the University of Vermont with a Bachelor of Science degree, *cum laude*. The labels on the file drawers read WRITING, RECORDS, LAB, MISC.

Before I could attempt to pick the cabinet lock, Jerry Smith said behind me, "This is a quiet apartment. Lath-and-plaster walls just soak up sound like a sponge." He was leaning casually in the doorway. "What are you looking for?" he asked.

"Fungus."

He laughed. "None growing in here. Come on into the living room and let's talk like civilized people."

He sat in the chair, I took the sofa. "I know you were up to something with Eva," I said.

He raised his eyebrows.

"And you shot her," I said. "I thought it was Darryl, but I was wrong. Why didn't you finish me off? Did you think I was dying already and there was no need for further effort? Or that if I thought it was Darryl that would get you off the hook?"

He shook his head and sighed. "You've lost me. I'm going to put on a pot of tea." I started to get up, but he motioned me back. "Your shoulder must bother you. I'll bring it in here."

While he tinkered in the kitchen I counted books. He had seventeen on his shelf dealing with mycology, the branch of biology that deals with fungi.

"Here's our tea," he said as he returned with a tray bearing two steaming mugs and three small brown bottles, each with a hand-lettered label. He picked up one and shook it, showing me that it contained a powder. "Fungus," he said. "OK, this fungus is famous in Chinese medicine. It's Cordyceps, and it lives on the cocooned larvae of moths and cicadas. It used to be horrendously expensive, but a few years ago scientists found a way to grow the fungus in a culture." He opened the bottle and tilted about half a teaspoonful of the powder into the cups.

He picked up a second bottle. "This one isn't a fungus but the root of a plant. Siberian Ginseng, or Eleutherococcus. Cordyceps is the ultimate Chinese tonic, Eleutherococcus the ultimate Russian one. You'll find the effects gentle but stimulating."

"You were in Eva's car when you killed Jeremiah," I said.

"He wasn't really my grandfather," Jerry said, stirring his tea. "I was adopted."

"You put the flare in his truck and shot at him?"

"That was Bill Grinder." Jerry smiled. "His phone in the shop call-forwards to his cell phone. Jeremiah never even considered that it could have been him."

"And Grinder shot at me in the cabin when Eva came to get those files."

"That was Eva's idea. She wanted to scope your place out and find out what you knew."

"What happened? How did Lauser get involved?"

"Bad luck. Benson saw me returning Eva's car. Lauser did work for them. He was supposed to scare me away from Eva, that's all." He grunted in soft laughter. "Benson and Lauser thought I was sleeping with her. They were wrong. I was doing business with her." His voice got louder. "Lauser was an idiot. He planned to go to the USDA about the mycorrhizae. Benson was an idiot, too. He was running scared and wanted to get his company away from GMOs. I told him I could fix it."

"You developed the pine fungus," I said.

"I did," he said softly. "It was part of my PhD dissertation, actually." He leaned forward, elbows on his knees. "Once I get it right, I can patent it and sell it for millions."

"Except it kills trees."

He glared at me. "The next iteration won't! It's a matter of fine-tuning. Benson financed my research, but he cut himself off from me. Whatever. I don't need his company. I'll sell the next patent for fifty million and Benson's company will go down the tubes."

"And I can't prove any of it."

"But it's good to know your guesses were right." He got up. "I'll be right back."

He went through the bedroom, into the bathroom, and I heard him urinating. I looked at the two mugs.

Don't interfere.

But I did a little fiddling.

The toilet flushed and I heard Jerry wash his hands. When he came back he said, "Much better." He sighed. "I spent all morning with the police. Two shootings at your cabin, one tore a chunk out of my grandfather's ear, got them all full of themselves." He saw I was holding my mug, and he winked and picked up his own. "Go ahead. You'll like the taste."

I could smell his tea, musty and sweet, with a faint hint of apple. He drank from his mug, first a taste, then throwing back nearly half of it. "Delicious."

I drank half the contents of mine, watching his smile as I looked over the rim of my cup.

We sat like old friends, drinking until both of us had nearly finished.

Then Jerry laughed. "You switched the mugs."

"Did I?"

He tenderly picked up the third brown bottle. "This is *Amanita phalloides*. The death cap. One of the deadliest fungi in existence. There is no antidote. It's also a strong hallucinogen. Before a victim dies, he gets a really wild trip. And this tincture has virtually no taste."

He set it down. "Of course, if I was going to poison one of the mugs, I would have poisoned mine. I could have been certain that you'd switch them when I was out of the room. I know you're clever. I know your instinct."

"Like you knew the cleverness and the instincts of your UVM advisor?"

"He poisoned himself."

"You know, Jerry, I don't believe that," I said. "I think he saw how crazy you are. I think he knew that letting you play around with genes was like letting a weak-minded twelve-year-old run around with dynamite and matches. I think he had you pretty well pegged."

His face had turned scarlet. "Summers was an old fool. He was afraid of nothing, afraid of shadows. He had me pegged? I had him nailed. And he poisoned himself."

"As I just poisoned myself by drinking this tea?"

The tension was ebbing out of him. He grinned, a sick, sly grin, the expression of a rabid fox. "You're too smart. You'd choose the cup that wasn't poisoned." He rubbed his eyes, still grinning. "But you outsmarted yourself, and you'll be dead in twenty minutes. I put a little bit of wormwood in the cup I gave you—it gives a distinct bitter flavor to the tea, but it's not at all toxic in such a tiny dose. Your tea was totally safe. And when I drank mine, I tasted the wormwood. You switched the cups, just like I knew you would."

His sick smile broadened, the smart little boy so proud that he'd figured out how to kill, so much smarter than anybody else in the world. He was a god, could control life and death, and even if his GMO experiments didn't work this time, and might even have destroyed every pine tree in the world, they'd work just fine the next time. Stupid humans; we'll never understand his true brilliance.

I leaned forward and poured the remainder of my mug into his. Clear water flowed out.

He blinked as if he were having trouble focusing. "I could have switched mugs," I said slowly and clearly. "Or I could have carried both to the kitchen, poured half of each down the drain, and put the rest together in one mug. And I could have rinsed the other one and filled it with plain tap water."

Jerry's red face was now very pale as he tried to get up, but he was shaking so violently he slipped sideways in the chair. I took my mug to the kitchen, rinsed and dried it, wiped it clean of fingerprints and put it up.

I think Jerry was trying to tell me something when I passed back through the living room, but whatever it was came out as mindless, gobbling, bubbling noises.

I let myself out.

25

ina's friend Elaine had long, wavy chestnut hair and big round wire-rimmed glasses. I guessed her at thirty, plus or minus three years. I liked her voice, a full, rich, modulated contralto, as though she worked in radio or theater, but she was a physician, with a one-woman medical practice in Barre, a nearby town. "God, it's turned cold again and it's snowing," Elaine said. "How long does this last?"

"It's February, and it's Vermont," Gina told her fondly. "Ask again in three months."

We'd kept our dinner date, sitting in a corner table in the Single Pebble, which very well may be the best Chinese restaurant in North America. With a pair of chopsticks I picked off my plate a thinly sliced shitake mushroom and shakily maneuvered it to my mouth.

"Give me a break," Elaine was complaining. "I haven't been here for a full year yet." She gave me a professional glance. "You're having some pain."

I was, but didn't think it showed. "It's not all that bad."

Then Gina's cell phone went off, a Beethoven melody. She made a face, answered it, covered her free ear with her hand

and murmured a few words. Her eyes grew wide and then she said, "Excuse me." She headed to the restrooms, away from the murmur of table conversation, with one palm still pressed against an ear.

"I hate those goddam things," Elaine said.

"All the inconveniences of home," I agreed.

Elaine took a delicate bite of food and gave me a speculative look. "So. Gina says you're a detective."

"Retired," I said. "Temporarily."

"Temporarily?"

"I'm thinking of starting my own agency. A small one." The mock eel was really delicious. I trapped another mushroom with my chopsticks.

"Isn't that—forgive me—an occupation that's kind of dangerous?"

"I don't think of it that way," I told her. "In school I was always the kid who tried to break up the fights. I never liked seeing bullies gang up on a little guy. I guess I haven't changed much."

"We're on a pretty big playground now," she said. "A lot of bullies out there. Sometimes you get hurt if you interfere."

I felt a small sharp pang, not from my wounded shoulder. "Sometimes," I said quietly, "somebody has to interfere." I drank some tea. "Somebody who is awake enough to know what's going on."

She looked at me with a faint, puzzled expression. Gina came hurrying back, her face heavy with news. I knew what she would say before she said it: some anonymous computer guy had flooded several different federal agencies with e-mails between Caleb Benson and Jerry Smith. She did say that, and more: Benson had just been taken into custody by federal marshals. The EPA was hurrying to a site in the woods to learn how much decontamination had to be done.

"I've got to go to work," she said. She punched in a number and said into her phone, "Hi, it's Gina. Listen, all hell's breaking loose. Can you meet me in the newsroom? And get Jerry. What? *Jesus!* Are you sure?"

She switched off the phone and looked at us with dazed eyes. She whispered, "Jerry Smith is dead. He poisoned himself."

Elaine put her hand on Gina's forearm. "Are you all right?"

Gina almost jerked at the gentle inquiry. In a taut voice, she said, "Yes. No. I don't know. I've got to get back to the newsroom."

"I'll drive," Elaine said. She gave me a pleading look.

"Go ahead. I'll settle the bill." I watched the two women walk out of the restaurant.

It was a lonely drive back to Northfield, along a snow-blurred highway. My shoulder throbbed abominably. Before I got there, a cop pulled me over and cited me for not having taillights. I'd have to get that fixed. Maybe Darryl would do it for me. He was a fair mechanic, and I still had a few of Jeremiah Smith's dollars. Maybe Darryl could settle down and do something he was halfway good at, maybe he could make something of himself. Marie needed a father. Wanda needed love.

And that made me think of Jerry, Eva, and Caleb. I brooded over the old triangle of corruption: money, sex, power. The primal stuff of the human condition. I did not look forward to spending the night alone in my cabin. It was haunted by too many memories, too much death. I knew with a certainty that I would lie there sleepless unless I drank myself into a stupor. I did not want to drink.

But when I made the turn onto the old logging road, something astonishing happened. At first it was just puffs and drifts of snow chasing each other through the headlight beams, traveling diagonally across my path, right to left. Sitting in the Jeep, I paused, like Frost's enchanted sled traveler, to watch the woods fill up with snow. And then in utter silence the first one emerged from the forest. And then another and another. And before my eyes a herd of a hundred, five hundred deer, crossed before me, many pausing and looking at me with gentle eyes. There couldn't be that many deer in Vermont, I thought.

And I somehow knew that if I climbed out of the Jeep they would all vanish and become a trick of the light, a secret of the night, no more than drifting wisps of snow. And in the morning light I would find no tracks, not a single one.

Something huge and dark brought up the end of the long procession, too far beyond the headlights' reach for me to see the Grandfather Bear shape.

I switched off the lights and sat in the Jeep for a few minutes more, feeling that I had been given a vision, a blessing, and perhaps even unearned forgiveness. Then I got out and headed uphill to the cabin.

I knew now that I'd be able to sleep.

ACKNOWLEDGMENTS

Thanks to David Heron of the USDA, Kirk Waterstripe and Charles Redon of Soil Foodweb Inc., Brian Halweil of Worldwatch Institute, and in particular Dr. Norman C. Ellstrand of the University of Texas for help and information on everything from genetics to mycorrhizae.

And to Dr. Elaine Ingham and Dr. Michael Holmes for discovering, back in the 1990s, the plan to release the genetically modified *Klebsiella* plant-root bacteria that almost killed the world—yes, it's a true story—and for Dr. Ingham coming on my radio show to share it. We ignore their warnings at great peril to ourselves. For more information, visit http://online.sfsu.edu/rone/GEessays/Klebsiellaplanticola.html or just run a web search on their names.

I was informed and inspired by listening to brilliant Abenaki storytelling by Joe Bruchac, and later by his son, Jesse Bruchac, on several public occasions in the late 1990s and early 2000s when I lived in Northfield and Montpelier, Vermont, and by the wonderful people at the Abenaki Center in Swanton. Any errors in this book about the Abenaki are entirely my responsibility, and I hope I have represented them respectfully. And it's worth noting that shortly after the point in time at which the book is set, in 2006, Vermont officially recognized the Abenaki.

Thanks to Hal and Shelley Cohen for sharing that decade's Vermont journey with us.

Thanks to Carol Bedrosian and Little Bear, Ari Ma'ayan, Kurt Kaltreider, and Lewis Mehl-Madrona, for all they've each taught me about Native American culture. And to authors Rupert Ross and the late Peter Farb for their books *Dancing with a Ghost* and *Man's Rise to Civilization*, respectively (among many others; these are exceptional).

Special thanks to Rob Kall for being such a good friend and sounding board on this book, and to Bill Gladstone for his brilliant work as my agent.

To Brad Strickland, one of the finest writers in print today, for decades of friendship and one of the finest editing jobs any author could ever ask for. Brad helped me shape this book into its current form.

To Anita Miller, Devon Freeny, and Kristi Gibson for finding all the nooks and crannies, plot points, and details that I'd overlooked and made no sense. To Mary Kravenas and Caitlin Eck for their work marketing and publicizing this book. And to Cynthia Sherry, Anita and Jordan Miller, and Academy Chicago Publishers and Chicago Review Press for bringing it into print.

DATE DUE

3/20		
6:29		
3		
8/7		
		PRINTED IN U.S.A.